WHAT I LIKE ABOUT YOU

A RESCUE MY HEART NOVEL

KAIT NOLAN

What I Like About You

Written and published by Kait Nolan

Cover design by Kait Nolan

Copyright 2019 Kait Nolan

AUTHOR'S NOTE: The following is a work of fiction. All people, places, and events are purely products of the author's imagination. Any resemblance to actual people, places, or events is entirely coincidental.

A LETTER TO READERS

Dear Reader,

This book is set in the Deep South. As such, it contains a great deal of colorful, colloquial, and occasionally grammatically incorrect language. This is a deliberate choice on my part as an author to most accurately represent the region where I have lived my entire life. This book also contains swearing and pre-marital sex between the lead couple, as those things are part of the realistic lives of characters of this generation, and of many of my readers.

If any of these things are not your cup of tea, please consider that you may not be the right audience for this book. There are scores of other books out there that are written with you in mind. In fact, I've got a list of some of my favorite authors who write on the sweeter side on my website at https://kaitnolan.com/on-the-sweeter-side/

If you choose to stick with me, I hope you enjoy!

Happy reading!

Kait

CHAPTER 1

Sebastian Donnelly shifted in the saddle, giving the chestnut mare a subtle nudge with his knee. After only a moment's hesitation, Gingersnap switched directions, resuming her trot around the training ring.

"There's a girl."

Her ears swiveled back toward the sound of his crooning voice, so he kept up a low patter of one-sided conversation as they continued to circle. She was attentive to every touch, every signal, every shift of his weight, and it was immensely satisfying that she did it out of a desire to please him rather than out of fear.

She'd come a long way in the eight months since she'd been rescued. No one looking at her now would know she'd spent the last few years of her life subjected to profound neglect and abuse. She'd put on weight, so her ribs no longer showed through. The coat that had been dull and matted on her arrival now shone with a gleam. The mane and tail he'd spent weeks detangling, as he slowly, methodically earned her trust, fluttered with the breeze of her movement. He'd waited months before going near her with a saddle and bridle, and longer still before trying to ride her. She hadn't been ready. But over the past few weeks, it had become clear that she'd had training before landing with the asshole who'd let her damn near starve to death. The sweet temperament he'd seen beneath the fear had emerged like daffodils in the spring, and Sebastian marveled that her spirit hadn't been fully broken.

This was the joy and the miracle of the work he did. The work that had saved his own broken spirit.

A flash of movement at the rail caused a hitch in Ginger's gait. Sebastian saw his stable girl climbing up so she could see better.

"She's looking fantastic!" At fifteen, Ari was bright, eager, and utterly besotted with all things equine. She'd been trading stable labor for additional riding lessons since the spring, so she was a familiar part of Sebastian's day.

"Coming along," he agreed, slowing the mare to a walk.

"Can I ride her?"

Sebastian shot her a look. All of his rescues had an assortment of behavioral issues he'd been working on since they came to the farm, and many weren't part of the group he used for lessons.

Ari folded her hands and put on her begging face. "Please? Just for a few minutes? I could stay on the lunge line."

He considered it. She'd proven herself a capable rider, quick to take instruction or correction, and Ginger was turning out to be a gentle, responsive mount. It might be a good fit.

Even as he thought it, the mare tensed beneath him and began to dance. Her ears twitched in agitation. Then he heard what she had.

Thunder.

It rolled over the land, echoing off the mountains that cupped this little pocket of paradise. As Ginger gave a little buck and twist, sidestepping across the ring, Sebastian ignored Ari, switching his full attention to his mount.

"Easy. Easy. Settle."

Tension crackled around her as he brought her in line. She quivered beneath him, nostrils flaring as he held her through another rumble of thunder. Her war between an instinct to flee

2

and a desire to please him was evident in the way she tossed her head, eyes rolling. Storms were a huge trigger for her, and the only way to overcome that trigger was to keep pulling it, making her face it. Given their exceptionally dry autumn, there'd been limited opportunity to work on it, so he had to take the chances as they came.

For another twenty minutes, he battled her fear, taking the mare through her paces, despite the incoming storm. Ginger's anxiety was a palpable thing, and Sebastian deliberately banked his own emotions, knowing she'd ultimately mirror him. He just had to remind her of that trust. When she hesitated, he coaxed her through. When she danced, he reminded her to follow his lead. And when the first fat drops of rain began to splatter, he relented, reining her in long enough to dismount. Stepping close, he laid a hand on her quivering neck. "It's all right. You're all right."

Ginger held for him, though it was clear in every tense muscle that she still wanted to bolt. Stripping the saddle as quickly as possible, he heaved it over a rail and led her to the adjacent pasture. There, he removed the bridle and set her loose. As the next boom of thunder rolled, the mare took off at a run, kicking up her back legs and galloping a wide circle of the pasture as the other horses looked on. A few were already plodding toward the three-walled shelter to get out of the rain.

Ari came to join him, hood up and hands shoved into the pockets of her coat against the cold December wind. "Think she'll ever get over her fear of storms?"

"Maybe someday. She's got a long way to go." He didn't know what had happened to the mare to instill this abject panic, but he'd learned early on that keeping her in the barn was a non-starter. It was a damned miracle she hadn't broken a leg in her terror the one time he'd tried. All in all, the entire herd did better when they weren't confined.

Sebastian and Ari both stared after Ginger for another couple of minutes, waiting until she'd run off her first burst of anxiety.

He couldn't stop the worry or the guilt that niggled. Had he done enough? Should she be further along? It was fruitless speculation. The mare was where she was. There were only so many hours in the day, and the reality was that many of his were tied up with the riding school. It was a necessary evil—one he hoped would eventually make his rescue program self-sustaining. But that was a long way off. For now, that meant more time with students and less time one-on-one with his rescues. Slower progress was still progress.

"Help you clean up?" Ari asked.

"Appreciate it." Sebastian hefted the saddle, while she grabbed the bridle, and they made their way to the barn. "You got a ride home?"

"Logan's taking me. Are you sure it's not a problem I won't be around for the next few days?"

Her earnestness amused him. "It's not every day your aunt gets married. It's fine. Logan's bringing in some extra help for dealing with the rest of the stock while he and Athena are away."

The man himself showed up as they were stowing gear in the tack room. "Looks like we're in for a gullywasher."

"Yep," Sebastian agreed. "Worst ought to be done before too late tonight, though."

Logan slung an arm around his soon-to-be niece. "You about finished, kiddo?"

"I need to grab my backpack from the house."

He jerked his head. "Go on and do that. I wanna try to get you home before the storm breaks."

When he continued to linger after Ari had run off, Sebastian knew he had something on his mind.

"Something up?"

"Well, I actually wanted to ask a favor."

"Is there something else you needed me to take care of, while you and Athena are gone on your honeymoon?"

"What? Oh, no. It's about the wedding itself. My college friend

Nick is one of my groomsmen, and he's not gonna be able to make it. His dad just had a heart attack this morning."

"That's terrible." *What does that have to do with me?*

"Yeah. It's looking like he's gonna be okay, but Nick doesn't want to leave him, and anyway it puts us one man short on my side. I was hoping you'd be willing to be a stand-in groomsman."

Sebastian blinked. "You want me to be in your wedding?"

Logan's mouth quirked up in a grin. "I know it's last minute and there's a monkey suit and all that. But I consider you a friend and it happens you're about Nick's build."

Sebastian wasn't exactly keen on getting up in the middle of all the wedding festivities. There was a reason he worked with horses instead of people. Still, he owed Logan a lot.

The man had taken on a handful of horses simply because there'd been a need and he'd had the space. With his hands already full from managing all the moving parts of his organic farm, he'd needed help. As a favor to their mutual friend, Porter, Logan had turned over the care of the horses to Sebastian, giving him a job, a home, and a new purpose—something that had been sorely lacking since he'd separated from the military. He'd fully supported Sebastian's expanded equine rescue efforts, going so far as to delegate a solid chunk of acreage and the original barn at Maxwell Farms to that purpose. Over the past eleven months, and through the joint labor of fully restoring that barn to be a working stable, he'd become a friend. He'd stood for Sebastian through some seriously dark days, and Sebastian was humbled to be asked to stand up with him on one of his brightest.

"I'd be honored, man."

He blew out a relieved breath. "You're saving my ass."

"Athena doesn't strike me as the type to give a shit whether the numbers are even or whatever." The award-winning chef would probably only care about the food, so long as they were married by the end of the day.

"She's not. My mama is. None of us want to deal with her fretting about what Emily Post etiquette thing isn't being met."

Clearly, Logan fell a very long way from that particular family tree.

"What do you need me to do?"

"The rehearsal is tomorrow at 4:30 up at the Methodist church. After that, we'll all be headed back to the inn for the rehearsal dinner. I'll see that you get the tux when you get there. Then it's just showing up at one on Saturday to do pictures before the ceremony and hanging out through the wedding and the reception after. Once the final group pictures are taken, you're free to bail."

"I'd planned to be at the wedding and reception anyway." He was a sucker for wedding cake, and rumor had it that Athena's pastry chef from her former Chicago restaurant was making it.

"Great. I really appreciate it, man." Logan offered his hand.

"No problem. Guess I'll be seeing you at 4:30 tomorrow."

As Logan headed up to the house to grab Ari and take her home, Sebastian rubbed a hand over his beard, noting it had gotten kind of scraggly. His horses didn't give a shit what he looked like, but he still had enough of his mama's voice in his head telling him what was right and proper. Looked like he'd need to clean up like civilized folks.

Laurel was so late.

She had reasonable faith that her big brother wouldn't excommunicate her from the wedding party and, from what she could tell, neither would his bride-to-be. But she knew perfectly well her mother would be having a hissy fit right about now, and nobody wanted to deal with that.

She'd been all set to get out the door of her Nashville apartment on time for the four-hour drive. But then The Call had come. The official job offer from Carson, Danvers, Herbert, and Pike up in New York. Roger Pike had called her himself to say how excited they all were to have her—as if it was a foregone conclusion that she'd accept the job, pending her upcoming graduation and the passing of the bar exam. It should have been. Newly-minted attorneys were not supposed to turn down offers from a top-five firm in the nation. Especially one with a starting salary like the one Pike had thrown at her. It had taken all of Laurel's considerable skill with words to navigate the conversation without giving an actual answer. Then another loss of precious time to come down from the post-call spaz so she was safe to drive.

She'd already been wound up about seeing her parents this weekend without having the spectre of this job hanging over the proceedings. She couldn't tell them. Wouldn't, even if she'd accepted. This weekend was about Logan and Athena, not her latest effort to please her father. But with every mile into the mountains, her shoulders tightened and her stomach churned.

What if Pike had told Dad himself? They'd clerked together once upon a time, long before Laurel's father had opened his own firm. She didn't think the job had been a result of nepotism—her class ranking at Vanderbilt spoke for itself. But she knew connections mattered. And she knew if she said no, the shock waves would have far-reaching repercussions. So, priority one was keeping the news under wraps so Logan and Athena had a drama-free wedding. If Dad already knew about the offer—well, she'd find a way to talk him down so it didn't turn the weekend into a shit show.

In the end, she pulled into the lot of the First Methodist Church, in tiny Eden's Ridge, Tennessee, a whopping forty-five minutes late. Whipping her Mini Cooper into a space, Laurel took a few seconds to run a brush through her hair and thumb two antacids off the roll in her purse before sprinting in her sensible heels to the front doors. In the vestibule, she paused to bring her breathing under control. Rosalind Maxwell would consider gasping for breath an unseemly insult to Laurel's already unforgivable tardiness.

Beyond the double doors leading into the sanctuary, she could hear the murmur of voices. Crap, they were probably wrapping up already. It wasn't like it took that long to practice walking down the aisle. When she thought she could speak without wheezing—really, she needed to carve out time to get back into the gym next semester—Laurel stepped inside. The voices stopped and all eyes turned to her. She resisted the urge to hunch her shoulders, instead pausing in the doorway, spine straight, shoulders back, all her debutante training coming to her aid.

If you're going to make an entrance, make an entrance.

"I'm so sorry I'm late. There was a pile-up on the I-40 on my way out of town." The lie rolled easily off her tongue. Traffic accidents fell under the heading of excuses her parents would accept. She could see them twisted around in a pew up front. Ignoring the moue of disappointment pinching her mother's pretty face, Laurel deliberately blanked her expression and strode down the red-carpeted aisle toward the assembled wedding party.

Grinning, Logan broke free of his position at the altar, long legs eating up the last several feet, so he could wrap her in a solid hug. "Good to see you, Pip."

She didn't bother rolling her eyes at the old nickname—short for Pipsqueak. Even in her heels, her brother towered over her. Instead, she burrowed in for a long moment, absorbing his natural calm. "Back atcha, big brother."

Hooking his arm around her shoulders, he led her the rest of the way to the front. "Everybody, I want y'all to meet my sister, Laurel."

She gave a little wave. As Logan began introductions to the rest of the wedding party, she was aware of her parents' disapproving glares.

"—remember Athena, and these are her sisters, Maggie,

Kennedy, and Pru. And this young lady with the sappy, romantic grin is Pru's daughter Ari. She likes to matchmake. Consider yourself warned."

Ari snorted. "Whatever. You're here, aren't you? That's a three-for-three success rate."

"I'm not sure you can claim credit for all of those," Kennedy pointed out.

The girl crossed her arms. "Who was it who gave you all a stern talking to when you were being idiots?"

Pru shot her daughter a look of affectionate reproof. "What she means is she's an incurably nosy and interfering romantic."

"I regret nothing," the teenager insisted.

Logan ruffled her hair. "Noted, Nosy. Moving on. This is our wedding planner, Cayla Black; my friend, Porter Ingram; and you remember Xander."

Did she ever. Her brother's former college roommate was still hot. He was also very married. To Kennedy, if she wasn't mistaken. They'd been high school sweethearts, once upon a time, and life had given them a second chance.

"Good to see you again, Xander. Congrats on your own nuptials."

He wrapped her in a quick hug. "Thanks. You grew up."

"Yeah, that happens. I'm all set to become a productive member of society and everything."

"So I hear. Never pegged you for law school as a kid."

Laurel's face felt stiff as she forced it into a smile. "It takes all kinds."

Logan continued with the introductions. "And this is Pru's husband, Flynn."

Flynn nodded with an expression every bit as impish as his daughter's. "A pleasure, to be sure." The greeting fell off his tongue with an unmistakable Irish brogue.

"This here is Master of Carbs, Athena's pal, Moses Lindsey. Moses is the genius behind our cake."

"I'm pretty sure that makes you the most popular guy at the wedding," Laurel told him.

His teeth flashed white against the burnished bronze of his face. "I aim to please."

"Please tell me there's chocolate." She folded her hands in supplication.

Moses jerked his head in Ari's direction. "Tiny over there already put in her order. There will be chocolate," he confirmed.

Laurel mimed a small fist pump. "You are a god among men." Chocolate cake would go a long way toward making up for the stress she'd endured this semester.

"And last but certainly not least, your escort, Sebastian Donnelly."

Laurel turned to the last groomsman and felt the faux, flirty smile slide right off her face. She froze there, hand partly outstretched as her gaze locked with a pair of deep, brown eyes. Her breath backed up in her lungs, and her heart slowed to a crawl.

His thick, dark hair was nearly black and just a little mussed, as if he'd combed it with his fingers straight from the shower. Broad shoulders tapered to a narrow waist and long, long legs. His button-down shirt clung to his arms in a way that told her he had plenty of muscle under the Oxford cloth, and she'd bet money there was a solid six-pack under there, too.

He stepped forward, taking her hand in his. "Hi."

As his long, callused fingers closed around hers, she could breathe again. A stillness seemed to flow out of him and into her, and all the running and the stressing and the anxiety that was her constant companion went quiet. Her breath came out on something very close to a sigh, the tension in her shoulders leeching out. In its absence, the pulse that had turned sluggish began to gallop. All the prospective polite banter evaporated from her brain, leaving her with only one thought: *Holy shit, you're gorgeous.*

She couldn't very well say that, though.

Words. I need words. I'm supposed to be good at those. Casting around for something to say, she blurted, "What happened to Nick?" Goofy, bespectacled Nick, who used to give her noogies and didn't leave her a tongue-tied mess of attraction.

"His dad had a heart attack, so Sebastian is standing in," Logan explained.

"Is his dad okay?" The question came automatically. Thank God, she sounded normal at least.

"Yeah, he came through surgery and woke up a few hours ago."

"Good," she murmured.

Sebastian still had her hand, still hadn't looked away. Why hadn't he moved? Why hadn't she? It seemed as if heat built between their palms, and Laurel wanted to bask in it.

She wasn't broken. After the last couple of years, she'd begun to think that Devon had been right. The last guy she'd tried dating, back in her first year of law school, he'd accused her of being a robot. She was driven and focused. In the grand scheme of trying to maintain her position at the top of her class through that brutal, first year of academic hazing, dating and sex hadn't been a priority. She hadn't been interested in anyone since. But standing here, palm-to-palm, with Sebastian Donnelly, she felt that interest roar to life like a furnace re-stoked. Heat rolled over her, and she could only pray she wasn't blushing.

One corner of his mouth quirked, as if he knew her brain wasn't firing on all cylinders. Christ, how was it legal for a man to have lips that sensual? The contrast to the neat, close-cropped beard did something to her long-dormant lady parts, and she couldn't help wondering what that beard would feel like on the sensitive skin of her inner thighs.

"—done with introductions, how about we do one last run through, so Laurel is up to speed, then we'll break for the rehearsal dinner. Okay?"

Jerking her attention to Cayla, Laurel pulled her hand free, resisting the urge to tuck it under her arm to savor the tingles from where he'd touched it. Her cheeks bloomed with warmth.

Good God, when was the last time she'd felt an attraction like this?

Pretty sure that would be never, she thought as she followed the other bridesmaids to the vestibule.

With half an ear, Laurel listened to the wedding planner reel off instructions. The rest of her was still back in the sanctuary, reliving the touch of Sebastian's hand. It wasn't the heat that drew her—though that had rocked her back plenty—it was the stillness. The same kind of calmness her brother had always exuded but... more, somehow. Rare and precious, that feeling called her more effectively than any siren. Taking her place in the line-up to walk down the aisle, she wondered what she had to do to get another hit.

CHAPTER 2

 he food was amazing. Sebastian figured that was par for the course when the bride was a chef and she'd brought in another of her chef buddies to cater the rehearsal dinner. It sure as hell beat whatever he usually threw together and ate standing up in the kitchen of his tiny cabin. In the Army, it had been drilled into him that food was fuel. But whatever magic combination of beef and vegetables this was—sourced from Logan's farm, Maxwell Organics, no doubt—was pure pleasure. Sebastian wondered if there was more in the kitchen.

Xander shoved back from the table. "Before we get on to dessert, we'd like to present Athena and Logan with a wedding gift from the whole family."

From the chair beside Sebastian, Ari muttered, "Oh, this is gonna be good."

She practically bounced in her seat, wicked humor dancing in those big brown eyes. At the arch of his brow, she pressed a finger to her lips.

When Xander came back a moment later with a large, flat parcel, wrapped in brown paper, Logan leaned back in his chair at the head of the table. "What are you up to, Kincaid?"

Expression deceptively bland, Xander propped the package, which measured maybe two feet by three feet, on one narrow edge. "Why don't you two come find out?"

Exchanging a look, the bride and groom abandoned their mostly empty plates to investigate.

Logan accepted the thing, running his hands over the edges. "Feels like a picture frame."

"Your powers of deduction have not failed you," Kennedy announced. "A house isn't a home without art, and we all collectively felt like this would make a fitting addition to your living room."

Athena shot Maggie and Pru a questioning glance. "You two were involved in this?"

"We were," Maggie answered.

"Then I guess we can trust it was in good taste." Athena reached out and unceremoniously ripped the brown paper.

From his position across the dining room, Sebastian couldn't see what the picture was, but Athena's face had frozen in shock. Logan tore the paper the rest of the way, revealing a fancy, heavy wood frame. He blinked a few times, the corner of his mouth twitching.

"Well, what are you waiting for?" Porter asked. "Show everybody."

Logan flipped the picture around. The image inside the professional frame was one of him and Athena standing in front of the house they shared at the farm. Logan was holding a pitchfork, and Athena stood to his left, wearing a chef's coat, with her hair bundled into a bun and a scowl on her face. Was that...flour dusted over her nose and hair? Something had grayed out the usually brown sweep of it. The photo had obviously been Photoshopped as a magnificent gag gift, poking fun at the farmer and the chef.

"I give you Eden's Ridge Gothic," Xander announced.

Logan's control cracked and he started to laugh. So did

everyone else. Everyone except for his parents. Lawrence Maxwell's brows drew down in forbidding disapproval, and his wife looked utterly appalled.

Sebastian decided Logan was either an alien or adopted. Either way, he wasn't anything like his parents. His mom was a prim, proper society wife. Sebastian knew the type. He'd seen them often enough where he'd grown up in Kentucky, usually on the arm of some rich guy, who paid for people like his mother to take care of their Derby contenders. Her husband was obviously accustomed to calling the shots. From everything Sebastian had observed this afternoon, the other man didn't appreciate the small, family wedding Athena and Logan had chosen or the non-country club setting for the rehearsal dinner and reception. Everything but the ceremony itself was being held at Athena's family's place, The Misfit Inn. Sebastian had a feeling that the only thing he'd find worse would be if festivities were being held out at the farm itself. It was clear they didn't understand their son or approve of his life choices. It was equally clear that the down-to-earth and relaxed Logan didn't give a shit. He was happy with his life and his choice of wife.

That wife-to-be looked less than amused. She shot daggers at Moses. "You said you destroyed that picture."

The big man crossed his arms, utterly unrepentant. "You really think I was gonna destroy evidence of what happened that time you tried to bake—"

"Stop!" She pointed in warning, but her own lips trembled with suppressed laughter. "What happens in the kitchen, stays in the kitchen."

"Yes, Chef," Moses rumbled, a chuckle underscoring the words.

"We figured you could hang it in a place of honor over the mantle," Flynn said.

Well, that just made the older Maxwells look like they smelled something nasty. If the bride and groom noticed, they didn't let on.

"Who on earth did you find to put all of this together?" Logan asked.

"I know a guy," Maggie admitted.

As the ribbing continued, Sebastian's gaze slid over to Laurel. She was a lot more buttoned up than her brother, though not stodgy with it like their parents. She had the look of a woman who needed to cut loose. Under other circumstances, Sebastian might have jumped at the chance to help her out with that. She'd put on a good front at the rehearsal, making all the right social remarks when she'd arrived. But she'd been strung tight as a bowstring, all but vibrating with tension. And just like one of his horses, she'd quieted at his touch. That fascinated him for reasons he didn't quite understand. It was a fascination he couldn't afford to indulge, despite the zing between them. She was Logan's sister. As a friend and also his boss, that was double the reason for Sebastian to keep his hands to himself. He needed all the reasons he could get because Laurel Maxwell was a beautiful creature with wounded eyes, and those were his kryptonite.

Her lips curved in a quiet smile as she watched her brother and Athena continue to joke around with their friends and family. There was a wealth of affection in her expression that told him she had none of her parents' reservations about Logan's choices. Sebastian wondered if she had just a little bit of envy for the ease of the whole Reynolds clan, compared to her own family. It couldn't have been easy coming up in a household with those parents and their undoubtedly high expectations.

Over the next few minutes, the table got cleared and dessert brought out. At the first bite, Sebastian forgot about seconds on dinner. Heaven was this creamy, chocolaty confection on a plate. Damn. Hanging out with chefs was going to ruin him for regular food.

"I would like to propose a toast." Lawrence lifted his glass.

All conversation died and attention turned in his direction. Like everybody else, Sebastian picked up his glass. He hoped the guy wasn't long-winded in toasts. He really wanted to get back to his dessert.

"To my baby girl."

What the hell?

Sebastian glanced at Laurel, who'd lost her small sign of happiness, her lips bowing into a frown.

"She's a hard worker and an exceptional student. She'll be graduating in the top one percent of her class at Vanderbilt Law School."

Laurel's fingers flexed on the stem of her glass, and two bright flags of color bloomed across her cheeks. She knew as well as everyone else that Logan's rehearsal dinner was not the time or place.

"Dad, what are you doing?" she murmured.

He's dissing your brother's choice to become a farmer, that's what. Sebastian gritted his teeth, knowing Logan wouldn't want a scene, but wishing he could do something to shut all this down.

"Today, all her hard work has finally paid off. She got a job with Carson, Danvers, Herbert, and Pike in New York, and I know she's going to go on to do great things."

Her back went ramrod straight, the last vestiges of relaxation evaporating as surprise, then resignation flickered over her face. "I haven't accepted the position yet. And this isn't—"

"Of course you'll accept. Roger is very excited to have you join the firm."

Around the room, the wedding party fidgeted in their seats.

Laurel had moved beyond embarrassed. The flush in her cheeks faded as her father continued to talk. The skin seemed to tighten over her cheekbones, emphasizing the angles of her face. A faint sheen of sweat popped on her brow. Sebastian kept a close eye on her, feeling his own pulse kick higher as he noted her respiration going fast and shallow.

Logan jumped into the breach, lifting his glass. "To my brilliant baby sister, who isn't a baby anymore. We're all exceptionally proud of you and wish you success in whatever you do."

As the chorus of awkward cheers faded, Laurel pushed back from the table. "Excuse me."

Sebastian counted down the seconds, while someone made a conversational volley about the dessert to try to get things back on track. At the one minute mark, he slipped out of his seat without a word and went in search of Laurel.

～

LAUREL STUMBLED OUTSIDE, into the cold night air. Everything was too close, too hot inside the inn, and she just needed some space to get her head on straight.

Dad knew about the job. Which meant that Pike had probably told him. Of course, to both of them, her acceptance was a foregone conclusion. She'd practically signed her life away when she'd applied for the job in the first place. She just hadn't realized it until the ink was already dry.

A sharp stab of pain speared through her chest. Laurel tried to hiss in a breath but couldn't seem to manage it. A thousand-pound weight had dropped onto her ribcage, keeping it from properly rising and falling. One hand went to her sternum to press and rub, as if that would somehow alleviate the ache. But it didn't. Not like it usually did. She'd had a milder version of this before, and it always went away, but this...this was so much worse. Her vision was starting to go spotty. Jesus, was she going to further ruin her brother's wedding by having some kind of a cardiac event because she couldn't be bothered to make time for a physical in the middle of the semester?

Large, warm hands closed around her upper arms from behind. Sebastian. Laurel didn't question that she recognized his touch without him saying a word. He steered her toward one of the chairs on the wraparound porch and nudged her into it.

"Sit before you fall. You need to breathe."

Her legs folded like a newborn foal's. "Having some trouble with that at the moment," she wheezed.

He knelt in front of her, those big hands circling her wrists, the tips of his fingers resting against her pulse points. His touch was electric, even in the midst of…whatever crisis this was.

"Look at me." His voice was firm and gentle.

Laurel lifted her gaze to his, appreciating for a moment that she could look her fill without feeling embarrassed. She'd had enough embarrassment tonight.

The porch light cast faint shadows on his face, sharpening the lines of his cheeks above the close-cropped beard. Her fingers itched to stroke it, to find out whether the hair would be soft or rough. His eyes were dark, focused entirely on her. What would it be like to have that kind of focus on her when she wasn't in the middle of a medical emergency?

"Match your breath to mine. In and out." He sucked in a slow breath, his broad shoulders rising.

She followed suit, feeling the unbearable pressure on her chest ease a fraction. They let out their synchronized breaths slowly, then did it all over again. With each inhale, she seemed to find more oxygen. With each exhale, she noticed more details about him. The breadth of his shoulders. The outline of his defined chest, visible in the way his shirt stretched across it. The coiled power in the body crouched at her feet. Something about that leashed capability did something to her, making her belly swoop and swoon. Or maybe that was his thumbs brushing the insides of her wrists, shooting little trails of lightning up her arms. That sensation was much more pleasant to think about than the pain in her chest, so she let her focus narrow in on the tingles and imagine what it might be like if he touched her somewhere beyond her wrists.

"You get panic attacks a lot?"

Laurel blinked, pulled out of the hazy, half fantasy. "Panic attacks? I don't get panic attacks."

"Pain in your chest, trouble breathing, racing pulse, clammy skin, possibly nausea, dizziness. How'm I doing?"

Clammy skin? Suddenly embarrassed, Laurel wondered if she should yank her hands away. Instead, she held herself still and answered the question. "Spot on...but...I don't feel panicked. I'm not afraid of anything."

"Anxiety presents itself in all kinds of ways."

She scowled a little. "You've been hanging around my brother too much." Logan, her brilliant big brother, who'd bucked family expectation to get his graduate degree in clinical psychology, before bailing on that, too, to become an organic farmer.

"As he is fond of saying, you can take the therapist out of the master's program..." Sebastian said it with the kind of ease that told her he'd been a target of Logan's occasional armchair psychologist routine. Somehow that made this easier.

"Yeah, yeah. I still don't understand why this would be hitting me now."

Sebastian angled his head, those dark eyes studying her. "Being used as a blunt instrument to bash your brother's choices probably didn't help matters."

This man was too observant by half. He'd been thrown into the deep end by standing in at this wedding, and he'd already zeroed in on their fucked up family dynamics. Wincing, Laurel closed her eyes, wishing that would wipe away the scene still playing on a loop in her head. "God. Dad has no shame. I can't believe he just did that. This is Logan's *wedding*. None of this is about me."

"For what it's worth, it's not you everybody's judging."

Laurel opened her eyes at that, noting the simple sincerity in Sebastian's expression.

"I feel like I should go apologize for him." And that would go over like a ton of bricks. "Except nobody calls out Lawrence Maxwell."

"You aren't your father's keeper," he said easily. "As to the rest, I'm getting the sense you're not too keen on the job your dad thinks you're going to accept."

That was putting it mildly. She began to think about the rock and hard place she was wedged into, where the choices were to be railroaded into a job and a life she was no longer sure she wanted, or to give up the accolades and approval she'd worked so hard to attain in favor of...what? She wasn't like her brother. She didn't have another plan. Law was all she knew. It was the only path she'd even considered. And now...now it felt like a cage door was swinging shut, trapping her.

That just kicked off the panic again. She recognized it now that Sebastian had pointed it out. Her breath went ragged.

Not wanting to descend into the depths of another attack, she focused on him again, on leaning into that feeling of attraction. Because he was still touching her, still stroking his thumbs gently over the insides of her wrists. She wasn't even sure he was aware of it. But she was. Oh, mercy, she was. And she wanted—needed—more of that contact. Slowly, she rotated her hands in his grip so she could curl her fingers around his wrists, linking them. His pulse seemed to jump against her skin. She was surprised to find it wasn't as slow as his rock-steady manner made it seem.

Was it possible this attraction wasn't one-sided?

Before she could process the idea of that, she heard footsteps on the porch. Ari circled the corner of the house just as Laurel yanked her hands away, folding them into her lap.

Ari went brows up at the sight of Sebastian still kneeling in front of her. "Sorry to interrupt. I got sent to check on you."

"I'm fine." The answer was automatic, but Laurel was surprised to find it was true. She could breathe again. Sebastian had effectively squashed the anxiety. For now, anyway.

Ari's lips pursed a little, as her gaze slid from Laurel to Sebastian, who rose smoothly to his feet. "If you hurry, there's extra dessert."

"Who do I have to arm wrestle for it?" Sebastian grinned and held out a hand to Laurel. "C'mon. You didn't actually get to eat your first helping."

She let him pull her to her feet, disappointed when he released her hand. She was the one who'd pulled away first. He'd been watching her closely enough to know she hadn't eaten? What did that even mean? As she preceded him into the house, trailing after Ari, she tucked that little detail away to pull out and examine later.

CHAPTER 3

*S*ebastian couldn't sleep. That in and of itself wasn't anything new. He and insomnia were close friends, and he'd lain awake so often, he knew every knot and swirl in the plank ceiling above his bed. But this time, it wasn't for the usual reasons. He wasn't thinking of war or death or those he'd lost on the field of battle and after. No, he was thinking of Laurel Maxwell. The absolutely off-limits woman he'd have on his arm in —he glanced at the clock—something like fourteen hours.

He hadn't been able to resist following her outside. Hadn't been able to stop himself from doing what he could to erase the panic he'd seen so clearly in her eyes. That vulnerability tugged at him in a way flirtation never could. It wasn't in him to ignore someone in need. So he'd intervened, touching her, breathing with her. Falling into those wide, hazel eyes. And now he couldn't stop remembering the petal soft skin of her wrists. The way her slim fingers had felt curling around his own wrists, forging a link between them.

No, not a link. It couldn't be a link because she was Logan's sister. Because she would be leaving the day after tomorrow.

And yet, he couldn't stop remembering how it felt to have her look at him with trust. He'd felt necessary, needed, a kind of validation he hadn't sought since his separation from the Army. He'd wanted, needed to press his mouth to hers, to watch those pretty eyes fall closed, to watch them open again hazed with want instead of worry. But even if she wasn't Logan's sister, he couldn't go there. He couldn't be her short-term distraction, her temporary knight. He'd known too many good men who'd let their hero complexes draw them down dangerous paths.

That way lay madness.

But touching her had felt so damned good.

Irritated and knowing he'd never find his way into unconsciousness, he gave up and dressed, shoving his feet into boots to head down to the barn. He'd check on his charges and work off some of this excess energy.

The night was colder than he'd expected, and he wished he'd thought to drag on more than a flannel shirt. His breath puffed out in clouds just barely illuminated by the crescent moon. Nothing stirred in the night. That utter stillness soaked into him, easing some of the restlessness he'd been struggling with. By the time he opened the side door of the barn, he felt calmer.

The interior was warm, full of the sweet, familiar scents of hay and leather, underscored with the musk of animals. This was the scent of his childhood. Of comfort. This was what had saved him after the Rangers. He hadn't known it could or would, and he could only be grateful that Porter had shoved him into this opportunity.

The sound of a low, female voice brought him up short. Stepping into the aisle, he saw Laurel at the other end, stroking a hand down Cas's nose. The gelding's expression could only be described as ecstasy. The moment she drew her hand back, he nudged her in the chest, hard enough she stumbled a bit.

"Demanding, aren't you?"

"That's Casanova. He thinks the attention of all ladies is his due."

24

Laurel startled with a little yip. "I didn't hear you come in."

"Sorry." He ambled toward her. "What are you doing up?"

Though her attention shifted to him, she stepped back to the horse and resumed her petting. "Couldn't sleep. I'm still in exam mode, and I haven't been able to convince my brain there's not something else I'm supposed to be doing."

He doubted that was the only thing, but he figured she'd talk about it if she felt like it, so he let it alone.

"You've spent time around horses before." So many people were leery of the big animals, but she didn't seem intimidated at all.

Her lips curved into an easy smile—a real smile, rather than the socially-appropriate one she'd been using all evening. This was the real woman. No artifice, no shields. And standing here in flannel pajama pants and a Vanderbilt sweatshirt, she was even more stunning than the put-together debutante he'd met earlier.

Danger. Danger, Will Robinson.

"Yeah. A long time ago. I was horse crazy like any little girl, and my parents indulged me for a while, expecting I'd get over the phase. They never would buy me my own horse. So that's on my bucket list someday. I haven't been riding in years."

Yeah, he could imagine the kinds of bullshit reasons they'd have given her. It wasn't appropriate. Wasn't ladylike. Didn't expand her resume.

If it hadn't been the middle of the damned night, he'd have saddled one of the horses and put her in the ring. She obviously missed it. Instead, he strolled over to lay a hand on Cas's neck himself.

"It gets in your blood and you never really forget."

She looked up at him in open curiosity. "Did you stop?"

Sebastian didn't people much. He preferred the company of his animals. And those people he did hang out with all knew his history, or enough of it to cover the big stuff. It was a new thing to be around someone who didn't know him at all. Didn't have any preconceived notions about who he was or what he'd been through. He could pick and choose what to tell her. What guy to be for this short, weekend entanglement.

"For a while I had a job that didn't allow me access. I didn't know how much I needed it until I got it back." Understatement of the century.

"How did you get into horses?"

"My mom. She worked for one of those horse farms everybody thinks of when they think about Kentucky, so I grew up around prize-winning Thoroughbreds and spent as much time in barns as I did our house."

Laurel beamed. "That sounds amazing."

"A lot of it was pretty awesome." Until it came to an end.

Her involuntary shiver pulled his brain away from that dark, mental path.

"It's freezing. You should be getting some sleep. It's an earlier day for you ladies tomorrow."

She studied him for a long moment, still absently scratching beneath Cas's forelock. "I'd rather keep talking. Unless you're headed to bed."

Her innocent words sent his brain down a merry, fantasy path involving her in his bed, where he found out exactly what was beneath that shapeless sweatshirt. His body stirred at the notion.

Nope. He needed to get that shit under control and fast. He ought to walk her back to the house. Instead, he found himself striding into the tack room to grab one of the blankets he kept for the nights he spent out here keeping watch on injured or sick horses. Shaking it out, he wrapped it around her shoulders, tugging the ends together like a big shawl. The motion inadvertently brought her a step closer to him, and he caught the faint, subtly floral scent of...what was that? Chamomile? Lavender? It reminded him of the herbal teas his mom used to drink.

Laurel reached up to clasp the edges of the blanket, her hand brushing his. "Thanks."

"Sure." He managed to withdraw without acting like he'd been scalded and nodded to a stack of square hay bales. "Want to sit?"

"Sure."

Sebastian sat first, back against the wall. He realized his mistake almost immediately when she sat beside him. They weren't touching, but it wouldn't take much to reach out and twine his fingers with hers. He was surprised by how much he wanted to. The dim interior of the barn in this silent stretch of night felt too intimate. Yet he didn't want to walk away and go back to his empty house.

Laurel let out a long, weighty sigh. "You were right, earlier."

He dragged his attention away from his desire to touch her and back to the conversation. "About what?"

"I don't want that job. It's what Dad wants me to do. What he's expected me to do from the moment I announced my intention to pursue the law. I didn't even know he knew about the offer. I was hoping he didn't, so I could avoid...well, exactly what happened."

He rolled his head toward her, catching the misery in her eyes. "What do you want?" It was a basic enough question, and one he doubted anyone else had asked her.

"To survive my last semester."

That wasn't the whole answer, certainly not the honest one. So he pushed, just a little, hoping to draw her out. "What else?"

She turned her head, and something other than misery came into her eyes. "To satisfy my curiosity."

Her voice was barely above a whisper and he found himself leaning closer to hear whatever she wanted to confide. "About what?"

"This." Lifting her face to his, she closed the distance between them.

Her lips were soft against his, but not tentative. It was a gentle question, and it shocked the hell out of him. For long moments, he couldn't do anything but sit there, stunned.

Laurel pulled back, a flush staining her cheeks. "Sorry." She looked away. "That was—"

Sebastian didn't allow himself to think about the wisdom of his actions. He could only focus on the need to know the taste and feel of her. Sliding his hand into her hair, he framed her face, bringing her gaze back to his. Her eyes were full of distress and a guarded hope.

"A surprise. It was a surprise." Then he lowered his mouth to hers.

Her hands came up to circle his wrists and he braced to pull away. Instead, she melted into him in a surrender that tore straight past what was left of his good sense. He was in so much trouble here, but hell if he could find the will to pull away.

Sweet. She was so damned sweet. And when he angled his head, tracing the seam of her lips with his tongue, she opened for him, pressing closer, as they both took the kiss deeper. Her hum of pleasure shot straight to his groin. Even as he fought not to drag her straight into his lap, she was shifting to straddle him. The weight of her against his erection almost had his eyes rolling back into his head.

Christ, she was going to kill him. And if she didn't, her brother surely would.

That reminder of the reasons he shouldn't be doing this provided a fresh injection of sanity. This was Logan's *sister*. The sister who didn't live here. Who he shouldn't—couldn't—pursue.

It took everything he had to gentle the kiss rather than gripping her hips and grinding against her. He eased them back, ending with short, nibbling kisses at each corner of her mouth before resting his brow against hers.

His breath was ragged. "Did that satisfy your curiosity?"

Laurel's voice, when she answered, was surprisingly steady. "Pretty sure it only gave me more questions."

Searching for some humor to lighten the mood, he pulled back to look at her. "Curiosity killed the cat."

"But satisfaction brought it back."

"What?" he laughed.

"That's the rest of that proverb. Everybody gets it wrong. So from my perspective, a healthy curiosity is a good thing."

As she grinned up at him, unabashed, Sebastian decided it was a damned good thing she was only here for the wedding because she was a temptation and a half. And one he couldn't afford to indulge in any further.

THANK GOD FOR WATERPROOF MASCARA.

From her position at the end of the line of bridesmaids, Laurel couldn't see Athena past all the standing guests. But the look on her brother's face as he caught the first glimpse of his bride had tears welling. He was rapt, eyes shining with more than simply joy. His throat worked, and the edges of his smile looked a little strained as he struggled to control his emotions. She hoped the photographer captured this moment so that Athena could remember it for the rest of their forever.

What would it be like to have someone look at her like that? Like she was the sun, moon, and stars. It would be easy to get drunk on that kind of adoration.

Athena reached the front of the aisle, radiant, as all brides ought to be. She wore no veil, and her long, golden brown hair was loose and curled, adorned only with some jeweled combs on either side. The simple column dress suited her down to the ground, as did the bouquet of calla lilies and greenery she carried.

Beside Laurel, Ari was grinning like the Cheshire Cat. On her other side, Pru was already crying, with an equally wide smile on her face as Athena paused, bending to kiss the cheek of her father, in his wheelchair at the head of the bride's side, before stepping to the altar and taking Logan's hand.

He radiated happiness and contentment. A part of Laurel

envied that. He'd bucked family tradition, gone his own way, and he was legitimately content with the life he'd built in a way very few people were. Everything about what he'd chosen was different than the life they'd led growing up. Different from what their parents had expected. What they'd been groomed for. How much of his happiness was rooted in defiance of all those implicit and explicit expectations?

As she stood in the sanctuary of the little church, listening to her brother make his vows to the woman who'd turned out to be his perfect match, she couldn't help but wonder if there was something more for her. Something else. Because she couldn't escape the probability that if she continued on her current path, she wouldn't find this. She wouldn't have time to because she'd be working as hard or harder to make partner as she had to maintain her academic standing in law school. Doing it for a few years was one thing, but for life? That didn't feel like an acceptable trade off.

Her gaze slid over to Sebastian, looking very 007 in his tux. Broad shoulders tapering down to a narrow waist, he stood perfectly still and balanced. No fidgeting, no shifting. Was that stillness something he'd honed in the Army or was it simply him? He hadn't told her he was former military, but Logan had mentioned it when he first took Sebastian on. She'd cared more about the fact that Logan was getting horses on the farm, but now she wondered about what had made Sebastian get out. If he felt her watching, he gave no sign. His focus remained on Athena and Logan, his expression appropriately serious.

Laurel hadn't seen him this morning. She wasn't sure if that was by his design or just because she'd been tied up with hair and makeup and pictures. There'd been no chance to talk to him alone. What would she even say? Some variation of "Please, kiss me again?"

Yeah, she could go for that. She could go for a lot more than that.

"I now pronounce you husband and wife. You may kiss the bride."

The minister's words sent her brain right back to the barn last night, and oh mercy, what a kiss that had been. Taking the lead was totally unlike her. And okay, maybe a little bit of it was to avoid talking about law school and the job thing because she'd been afraid to really consider her answer. But more, she'd been wondering what he'd taste like and whether that sizzle she felt every time he touched her would translate to a kiss.

Boy had it. And it might have led to more if Sebastian hadn't slowed them down. He pulled her out of her head, out of herself, and that was both exhilarating and dangerous. Better one of them had some good sense, she supposed. But it was hard not to feel a little regret. If last night had done anything, it was to shine a light on the total lack of closeness and intimacy in her life. She'd been reduced to little more than the robot Devon had accused her of being. She'd more than enjoyed the reminder that she was still a flesh and blood woman.

Blinking, Sebastian's face came into focus. Realizing he was waiting for her at the center of the aisle to escort her for the recessional, she propelled herself into motion, taking the few steps to close the distance and slipping her hand through the crook in his arm. His biceps strained beneath the tux jacket, and it took all of her self restraint not to run her hands up and down the glory of his arms. Every step beside him was a pleasure, as she soaked in his nearness and heat.

All too soon, they reached the end of the aisle and got caught up in post-wedding chaos. They separated, each moving to perform their respective tasks. Laurel paused at the window, looking out the front of the church as Logan and Athena got into the car they'd take to the reception back at the inn.

Ari squeezed in beside her and heaved a gusty sigh. "Don't you just love weddings?"

It was hard to be anything but amused at the girl's open romanticism. "I like this one. I'm happy Logan's happy."

"And just think. We're all here today because they hooked up at Kennedy and Xander's wedding."

Laurel choked on a laugh. "What? I thought they got together last spring."

"Well they did. But they had a fling at Kennedy and Xander's wedding first." Ari shot her a significant look. "Weddings are good for that."

Heat flamed in Laurel's cheeks. She knew the girl was waiting for her to look at Sebastian, who was somewhere across the vestibule, but she didn't give in to the urge. "You're incorrigible."

That irrepressible grin flashed. "So my mother often says. Doesn't mean I'm not right."

Someone called Ari's name.

"Coming!"

As she disappeared, Laurel was left flummoxed and irritated. Because, of course, now she was thinking about a wedding fling.

Did she want Sebastian? Without question. She wouldn't have kissed him, wouldn't have taken it as far as she had if she didn't. They had explosive chemistry, and he was far from indifferent to her. She had a feeling that if he hadn't been interested, he wouldn't have had a problem shutting her down. No, the want was not in question.

But would one night be enough for her?

She wanted it to be. Wanted to be a little wild and crazy for once, to have that experience to pull out and dream about when she went back to her normal life. But she knew she'd be lying to herself. One night with him would just make her want more, and she was supposed to leave in the morning.

Before she'd come, she'd been glad it would be a quick trip. Less time around her parents to stress. But now... The whole idea of leaving was depressing. The entire family was meant to reconvene at the farm for Christmas, when Athena and Logan got back from their honeymoon. But that would be just another opportunity for Dad to put his thumbscrews to use on her about the job.

She wished she just had more time at the farm. Interactions with her parents aside, she'd been more relaxed since she'd come to Eden's Ridge than she had in months back in Nashville. Here in the cool mountain air, she thought maybe she could finally decompress a little. Was it so wrong to want to breathe for a bit? To have a taste of the life that suited her brother so well?

As she began to gather up flowers to take back to the reception, an idea began to percolate. Maybe, just maybe, Logan could give her exactly what she needed. She just had to corner him and his bride at the reception.

CHAPTER 4

"You doing okay? Crowd getting to you?"

At one time, the concern in Porter's voice would've rankled. It was a mark of how far Sebastian had come that he didn't pop off with some sarcastic remark about not needing a babysitter. Like the rest of their band of brothers, he'd been a surly bastard when he separated from the Army. Nice to know he'd added a little veneer of civility. "Nah. Just people watching and trying to figure out how long I have to wait before snagging another piece of cake."

Which was true. If he was also cataloging his position relative to Laurel's so he could relocate before she cornered him to dance, well, Porter didn't need to know that.

She was pure temptation in the strapless, emerald green bridesmaid's dress that clung to her curves in a way that made his palms itch. Her dark hair was swept up, baring her neck and the soft, creamy skin of delicate shoulders. It was hard not to think about tasting her there, wondering what sound she might make if he gently sank his teeth into that tender spot where her neck met her shoulder. She was picture perfect and perfectly edible, so elegantly packaged that all he wanted to do was drag her into a dark corner and start mussing her all up.

But he wasn't about to do that, which was why he was engaging his Army Ranger skills to hide in plain sight. The inn wasn't that big, and the guest list wasn't so large that it was easy to blend into it, but Sebastian knew how to navigate covert operations. Skills he never thought he'd use to avoid a woman—especially not a beautiful woman he ached to have in his arms again.

Thinking of her, that sweet, natural, unedited beauty he found he preferred even to this portrait-worthy perfection, thinking of the weight of her in his lap, the scent of her skin, the hungry slide of her tongue actually made him weak in the knees.

But she was not for him.

He'd avoided female entanglements since he'd come to the Ridge—even the short-term, itch-scratching variety. There'd been interest from more than a few women. It was a small town, and he qualified as fresh meat, as it were. He hadn't reciprocated because his head hadn't been screwed on straight, and until that was sorted, he had no business pursuing anything with anybody. Especially not the much younger sister of his friend and boss. She deserved better than a broken-down soldier still working on getting his life together. And anyway, she'd be gone the day after tomorrow.

It was a fine line he was walking, saving himself from temptation without being an obvious asshole who left her thinking he regretted last night's kiss. That mind-blowing, hot-as-hell kiss that had been on repeat in his brain since they'd stopped.

"—expect we'll be doing this again sometime next year."

Sebastian tuned back into the conversation, wondering what he'd missed. Rather than admit he hadn't been paying attention, he made a grunt of agreement.

"How long do you think Harrison will wait before getting Ivy down the aisle?" Porter asked.

Next to Porter, Harrison Wilkes was the member of their

group who'd been out the longest. Last winter he'd rescued a woman whose car had spun out and crashed through a guardrail. He'd rappelled halfway down the mountain and ended up finding the love of his life.

Sebastian sipped at his beer. "Ty's got money down that he'll propose on New Year's. I think he'll do it on the anniversary of the day they met."

Porter crossed his arms. "My money's with you. Harrison's sentimental like that."

"Don't let him hear you say that. He might have to wrestle to prove his manhood. What about you?" Sebastian glanced across the room to the woman who'd always held Porter's heart.

Porter's face softened as he followed Sebastian's gaze to Maggie. "I'd marry her right now if that's what she wanted. But we'll get there. Sooner rather than later, if I get my way."

"I wish you luck, brother."

"When are you gonna get back out there?"

Sebastian arched a brow. "You going all matchmaker on me? I thought that was Ari's department."

"It's a natural enough question. You've settled into life here. Seems like a woman's the next logical step."

"There are some available should I want one."

"Which you haven't or I'd have heard about it."

"Only because Ty and Harrison gossip like little girls. I don't kiss and tell."

"So you've been kissing?" Porter's face lit with interest.

"Shouldn't we be braiding each other's hair or painting nails while you ask that? There's nothing to tell." God knew, recounting any of last night, even if he were so inclined, would have him popping a woody right here in the middle of all the guests. That was the last thing he needed.

Before Porter could continue his nosy-ass line of questioning, Logan strode up. "Sebastian. Just the man I was looking for."

Sebastian offered his hand. "Congratulations man. I hope you and Athena will be very happy."

Logan's smile practically lit up the room. "Already are. We're looking forward to getting away for a bit. Ten whole days, where I'm not having to wake up to feed livestock and the only thing I have to focus on is my wife, sounds like pretty much the best thing ever. A chance to really relax before we come home and have to scramble to get the place all duded up for Christmas. We're less than thrilled about that part, but that's what happens when you have an almost Christmas wedding."

"Can't blame you there. Where are y'all going?"

"Ponderosa Resort and Ranch. Some big luxury ranch resort out in Oregon. Athena's friend, Sean Bracelyn—the chef who flew in to do all the food for the rehearsal dinner and the reception— it's his family's place. We'll be headed out first thing in the morning to catch our flight."

"Were there some last-minute instructions you wanted to give me?"

"Oh, no. I just had one more favor to ask."

Feeling more than a little guilty for the naked thoughts he'd been having about Laurel, Sebastian just nodded. "Sure. Lay it on me."

"I'd like you to keep an eye on my sister."

He almost choked on his beer. "Pardon?"

"Laurel's had a rough semester, so she's going to stick around the farm to pup-sit Bo and Peep. Which really just means spoil them rotten and chillax a bit, while we're gone." Logan glanced across the room to where Laurel was in deep discussion with Maggie about something. "I'm worried about her. She says everything's fine, but I can't shake the feeling that something's off."

Sebastian already had a good sense of what, but it wasn't his place to say anything. He didn't know how close Laurel and Logan actually were. If she wanted him to know her business, she'd tell him herself.

"Anyway, I won't get the chance to find out until we get back, so if you could just touch base with her, in case she needs anything, I'd appreciate it."

He does not mean second, third, or home bases, dumbass.

Ten more days with Laurel, with nobody around to act as a buffer? His already suffering libido roared. Struggling to mask his reaction, he tipped back his IPA to wet a suddenly dry throat. "Sure, I can check in on her."

"Good." Logan's face eased to a relieved smile. "You might get some free labor out of it. She used to be seriously into horses when she was younger. I bet she'd love the chance to go for a ride."

She could save the horse and just ride me.

Aware of Porter's sharp gaze on his face, Sebastian could only nod. He lost the next few lines of conversation as he struggled to banish *that* image from his brain.

As Logan strode away, Porter's mouth quirked in amusement. "Oh brother, you are in serious trouble."

Don't I know it.

"Did you hear about Hugh Saunders?"

Laurel struggled to get her not-totally-caffeinated brain to fire. After the late night with the reception and the early morning seeing off the newlyweds, she was too damned tired to figure out why was her mother was bringing up the son of some of their country club friends. "I haven't seen Hugh since we graduated high school. Isn't he in med school now?"

"He *was*." Rosalind drew out the final syllable like a delicious piece of taffy, not that she'd ever admit to how much she adored gossip.

Knowing her part in all this, Laurel took the bait. "Was?"

Her father shook his head in disgust. "Ungrateful boy up and quit in the middle of his third year. He dropped out of *Harvard*. And not even because he was doing poorly. He just had some fool identity crisis and has gone to 'find himself' or some such."

Laurel could well imagine the kind of pressure Hugh had been under at an Ivy League med school. Dropping out couldn't have been an easy decision. "Maybe he realized he didn't want to be a doctor."

"He should've figured that out before his parents shelled out three hundred thousand dollars for that education. I don't blame Edward for disowning him."

"They *disowned him?*" Laurel demanded.

"Of course." Her father set his coffee mug down with the declarative thwack of a gavel—the Honorable Lawrence Maxwell, at the breakfast table, at least. "We were generous not to do that with Logan."

A chill skated down her spine and coalesced like a ball of lead in her stomach. She remembered the fallout from World War III, otherwise known as Logan's announcement he was quitting grad school to become a farmer. Their parents had been furious. But she'd never had a clue that they'd considered cutting him off from the family. This little story was a timely reminder of the possible outcome if she didn't live up to expectations. Laurel clutched her coffee mug a little tighter, as if the lingering warmth would somehow soak into her palms and soothe the fresh worry that spread like creeping frost through her body. She needed to get the hell away from this conversation before she slid into another panic attack or broke down and said something they'd all regret.

"Shouldn't y'all be getting on the road? It's a long drive back to Memphis." *Smooth segue, Laurel.*

If her parents noted the abrupt change in subject, neither gave any indication.

Lawrence drained the last of his coffee and shoved back from the table. "You're right. I'll go get the suitcases."

As her father disappeared upstairs, Laurel stayed where she was.

"Are you okay, sweetheart?" Rosalind asked.

I've just realized I'm caught between a rock and a flaming hot grill. I'm just peachy. "I'm fine. I was just thinking about Hugh. That's terrible about his family."

"It's a sad situation for sure." She stroked a hand over Laurel's hair. "Not everyone can have a child as bright and dedicated as you. We're grateful and proud of you every day. I hope you know that."

Laurel managed a smile and hoped like hell it didn't look like a bad case of rictus. "I know, Mom."

It took another twenty minutes to make sure the car was loaded and to do a last sweep of the house for forgotten toiletries, but at last, she hugged her parents, choking back the anxiety that wanted to crawl up her throat and through her chest like mutant vines in a horror movie. "Drive safe. Let me know when you get home."

Roslind squeezed her shoulders. "That's our line."

"Turnabout is fair play. I'll see you in a couple of weeks for Christmas."

"Enjoy your vacation," Lawrence told her. "Next semester will be busy busy, with the last of your classes and studying for the New York bar."

Laurel made a noncommittal noise.

As her parents climbed into the car, she called for Bo and Peep, her brother's faithful border collies. The pair raced over, plunking down on either side of where she sat on the porch steps. She wrapped her arms around them to keep them in place as her parents drove away. Long after their car had disappeared, she stayed where she was, feeling some of the tension drain away as the dogs leaned in, nuzzling her face, her hair.

Still more than a little shaky, she released the dogs and wandered down to the stables. She didn't want to think too hard about the fact that being upset had her instinctively arrowing toward Sebastian. She just...wanted to see him. He was a distraction, one she wanted to get to know better in pretty much every way possible.

It was a brisk, beautiful morning, with cloudless blue skies. Bo and Peep danced around her, bumping each other's shoulders as they streaked ahead and raced back. In the distance, a lone figure pivoted in the paddock, as a bay horse with two white socks circled on a lunge line. She recognized Sebastian long before she got close enough to make out his features. He wore a cowboy hat and well-worn jeans. Despite the cold, he hadn't bothered with a coat.

Leaning against the top rail, she took in the flex of muscles in his back—and backside—as he continued to turn. The man really was a gorgeous specimen. Seeing him like this, in his element, was ticking off all kinds of boxes for her. Foolishly, she thought of Jim Craig, the hero of *The Man From Snowy River,* which had been her favorite movie growing up. He'd been her first celebrity crush. And yeah, okay, that had been as much about the horses as the man. She'd been a typical horse-crazy tween and teen. But she'd never drooled over any of her instructors the way she was drooling over Sebastian right now. That was absolutely preferable to think about instead of the trouble with her dad.

"Parents get off okay?"

Stepping on the bottom rail, Laurel pushed herself up so she could see better. "Finally."

In a low, crooning voice, he slowed the bay to a walk and glanced her way. "Dad giving you grief again?"

Of course, he'd pick up on the tension in just her voice. This man seemed to be able to read her like a book. Laurel offered up a helpless shrug. What could she say?

"I've got a cure for that. Give me just a minute to finish up with Sassy."

She perked up. With any luck, his cure would involve his lips on her lips. She hadn't been able to stop thinking about that kiss. And maybe she'd have tried doing something about that last night, but with Ari's less-than-subtle suggestion hanging over her head, she'd been afraid Sebastian would think she was desperate or…something.

The ball is in your court, cowboy.

Sebastian cooled the mare for a few more minutes, before gathering up the lunge line and leading her over to a gate. As he unclipped the lead from her bridle, Sassy playfully bumped her head against his shoulder in a move that couldn't be interpreted as anything but flirtatious. It made him laugh. The sound of it, unfettered and rich, rolled over Laurel like warm molasses. He had a really great laugh.

"Go play, pretty girl. You've earned it." With a light slap on her rump, Sebastian sent Sassy into the pasture.

Shutting the gate after her, he crossed the paddock to Laurel, ducking through the rails right beside her. From where she still stood on the bottom, they were eye-to-eye. She thought maybe he'd step in or bodily help her down—something to acknowledge this snapping tension between them. Instead he studied her face for a long moment, his face inscrutable, before jerking his head toward the barn. "C'mon."

Okay, not going to be making out right this second. He probably has actual work to do after being tied up with wedding stuff all yesterday.

He was already half-a-dozen strides ahead of her before she leapt down to follow. Inside the barn, he led her down the aisle to a stall on the end.

"Hey gorgeous."

As Laurel caught up, a chestnut head poked over the stall door, stretching out for pets. Her ears tipped toward Sebastian, and he continued to croon nonsense compliments and scratch under the animal's chin.

"Are they all in love with you?"

Sebastian chuckled. "Most of the horses we have here are

rescues. A lot of them came from some pretty shitty conditions, and they're grateful to be here. I'm the one who does most of the care-taking, so yeah, several of them are fond of me." He kissed the chestnut's nose.

"I'd be careful if I were you. Sassy might get jealous."

"This little beauty is Gingersnap. Ginger for short. I got her back in the spring after a judge had her and another mare removed from their former owner for profound neglect. She was in pretty rough shape, and I wasn't sure if she'd make it. But she decided she wasn't ready to give up yet, and she's turned into a loving little thing."

Laurel eased up, holding out her hand for Ginger to sniff. "Poor baby. I'm glad she has you now. How did you get into all this? The rescuing?"

"Fell into it, actually. The first couple of rescues weren't me. There was a need and your brother had barn space. He mostly pastured them. When the next three came, he realized he'd need some help. Porter knew I was at loose ends and that I'd grown up with horses, so he did a little employment matchmaking. I don't think either Logan or I expected it to turn into this, but there's a need and, once word got out, we became the go-to place. Your brother never meant for things to get this big, but he's too damned nice a guy to turn anybody away."

Something in his expression made Laurel wonder if he was still talking about the horses or if he was thinking of himself.

"I've rehabbed and sold a couple of horses along the way, but it's a long way from being profitable. I started the riding school as a means of off-setting the cost."

With sixteen horses, she could imagine that wasn't an insignificant amount. Her brother wouldn't be in this for the profit, and she sensed Sebastian wasn't either.

So maybe profit isn't the answer.

She filed that away to think about later.

"Which part do you like best?"

"Definitely working with the rescues. Earning their trust again. And some of them, like Ginger here, that took a while. There are a lot of behavioral issues I'm working to correct. But Ginger...she's an absolute sucker for being groomed. Probably because she wasn't for so long. So my prescription for that lingering storm cloud over your head is to give her a good rubdown and grooming. It'll make you both happy."

So she wasn't going to be getting her hands on *him* again just now. That was fine. Reaching out, Laurel stroked a hand down Ginger's neck, bringing it up again to scratch under her chin the way Sebastian had. "How 'bout it, Ginger? You want a little beauty treatment?"

She took the horse's lean into her touch as a yes.

"I'll go grab the grooming bucket, while you two get to know each other."

Laurel and Ginger both watched as he strode down the aisle to the tack room.

"It's a nice view, isn't it?" Laurel murmured.

Ginger gave a wiffle of agreement.

Sebastian came back a minute later with the grooming tools. Setting the bucket aside, he opened the stall door and led Ginger out by the halter, walking her to an open sort of bay area, with two dangling lead ropes. He clipped one on either side of her halter. "You said it's been a while. You remember how to do this?"

Laurel fished the curry comb out of the grooming bucket and went to work, eliciting a long, satisfied groan from the mare. "Just like riding a bike."

"I'll leave you to it. Got my first lesson in five minutes." And then he was gone.

"Well, okay then." Laurel leaned to look Ginger in the eye. "A man of few words, isn't he?"

The monotony of grooming was soothing. As she worked Ginger over with long, slow strokes, the tension that had lodged in her shoulders during breakfast began to unravel.

She didn't need her pseudo-psychologist brother to tell her that all this anxiety was tied to their father and his expectations. Once upon a time she'd shared those expectations, had the same goals. Or maybe she'd just wanted what they represented. His acceptance and approval. It seemed she'd been chasing that her whole life.

Would she have made a different choice if she'd known the cost? She had no idea. All she knew at this moment was that she desperately needed to decompress from the semester—and really the last several years. Maybe if she could manage that over the next ten days, she'd be able to think clearly and make a decision about what to do.

By the time she began easing a comb through Ginger's mane, the mare's coat gleamed and Laurel felt almost relaxed again.

"She looks good."

Laurel yelped at the sound of Sebastian's voice from behind. "Jesus, Mary, and Joseph, are you trying to give me a heart attack?"

Ginger shifted, grumbling her displeasure at the interruption.

Sebastian's mouth quirked and he reached past her to stroke a hand down the horse's flank to soothe, which put him right up in Laurel's personal space. He smelled delicious. Like sweet hay and horse and leather. His sleeves were rolled up now, revealing those muscled forearms, lightly dusted with dark hair. She remembered the feel of those arms beneath her hands as he'd kissed her and looked up to find him staring at her lips.

Finally.

Tension crackling along her skin, Laurel stepped into him, lifting a hand to his chest and tipping her head up.

On a swallow, Sebastian stepped back, out of reach. The sudden space was like being doused in ice water.

For a moment, Laurel considered giving in to the burn of embarrassment and pretending it hadn't happened. But she was here for the next week and a half, and that meant they were going to run into each other. She knew what she'd hoped for when she'd asked Logan if she could stay. If Sebastian wasn't on the same page, she'd rather know now and save herself further mortification from chasing someone who didn't want to be chased.

Lowering her hand slowly, as if he hadn't just embarrassed the hell out of her, she met his gaze. "Have I misread the situation here? I thought, after the other night, that we had a mutual attraction going on. Is that not the case?"

That was totally the case. Laurel wasn't blind. He couldn't have kissed her like that if he wasn't attracted. But she'd give him a chance to explain.

Sebastian scrubbed a hand over the back of his neck. "The other night shouldn't have happened."

As she was trying to decide whether to be insulted by that, another thought wormed its way into her brain. "Are you with someone else?"

"No." Before the relief could even hit, he continued, "But your brother is my friend and my boss."

What the hell did this have to do with Logan? Shifting instinctually into interrogation mode she arched a brow. "Did Logan warn you off me, or is this your own sense of honor getting in the way? Because my brother is many things, but the over-protective Neanderthal is not one of them. He knows I'm a grown woman and can make my own decisions about who I do or do not get involved with."

His head kicked back in surprise. "Well, you're direct, aren't you?"

"I think our kiss the other night proved that in spades. I find life is simpler when you can cut to the heart of the matter." She ignored the little voice in her head that said she was a bit of a hypocrite since she was doing everything but that with her family. They were complicated. This attraction was simple. Or should be.

Sebastian sucked in a slow breath, looking around the barn, as if that was going to provide some kind of inspiration for what the hell to say. "No, he didn't warn me off. But he asked me to keep an eye on you. He's trusting me with you."

Oh for the love of...

Laurel dragged in her own measured breath, trying to get a handle on the burst of raw temper. She was well-accustomed to the Logan's-little-sister box. For so long it had meant coming second to her brother in her own family. But to get the same damned thing from Sebastian felt like a betrayal of whatever tenuous connection they'd built. And for what? Because he was afraid?

Screw this.

"You know, you're over here spouting Guy Code that thou shalt not get involved with thy friend's little sister, but the fact is, whatever does or doesn't happen between us has nothing to do with my brother. You're not protecting me by holding back, and you're not protecting your friendship with Logan, because that's not who he is. That means you're protecting yourself. And that's fine. It's certainly your right. I won't force the issue." Snatching up the bucket, she held it to her chest and looked him dead in the eye. "But maybe you should give some thought to exactly what it is you're protecting yourself from, Sebastian. You don't have to be honest with me, but I suggest you be honest with yourself."

With that closing argument delivered, she walked away.

CHAPTER 5

"Shit." Sebastian stared after Laurel, one hand still on Ginger's flank, reeling as if she'd sucker punched him.

He'd thought he could just ignore the attraction, avoid acting on it, and things would be fine. He hadn't counted on her calling him out. And he sure as hell hadn't expected her to put it all back on him. That was...uncomfortable. It made him realize his avoidance tactic depended upon her feeling like all this was her fault. That made him a coward and an asshole. He'd spent too much of his life trying not to be those things to let this stand. Turning Ginger out to pasture, he sucked it up and headed to the big house to find her and apologize.

The front door was, as usual, unlocked. He slipped inside, striding toward the kitchen in the back, where he heard the sound of water and low strains of music.

Her back was to him, her hands thrust into the sink of soapy water. All that rich, brown hair was bundled into a messy knot, exposing the length of her slender neck. For a moment he could only stare, imagining what it would be like to slip his arms around her and press a kiss to her nape, feel the length of her body pulled flush against him. The image stirred him more than he wanted.

Adjusting his jeans, he stepped into the room. "Laurel."

On a little shriek, she half turned and a plate slipped out of her soapy hand. As it shattered against the wood floor, she hopped back on bare feet, trying to get away from the shrapnel. "Ow!"

Sebastian leapt across the room to scoop her out of harm's way. He set her on a stretch of counter. Her hands, still soapy, clutched at his shoulders, and his fingers curled tighter around her hips. He wanted to step into the V of her thighs and take that smart mouth. To lose himself in the taste and feel of her. And from the way her pupils dilated and her cheeks flushed, she'd be on board. She'd been clear enough, hadn't she? This was why he'd avoided touching her again. Because once he started, he didn't want to stop.

But he didn't have any business pursuing those things with her.

Forcing himself to release her, he made his voice light. "You okay?"

"Christ Almighty, do you always walk like a damned cat?"

His lips curved at her breathless indignation. "You're a jumpy thing, aren't you? I didn't mean to startle you."

Her brows drew down into an adorable scowl that did nothing to dim the frustrated lust simmering in his blood. "I'm going to put a bell on you."

"There are probably some sleigh bells around here somewhere. Let's see about this foot."

"It's fine. I didn't step on anything. I just got caught in the crossfire."

Examining the cut himself, he decided she was right. He handed her a paper towel to press to the wound. "Here. Put some pressure on it, and I'll clean this up."

Sebastian felt her eyes on him as he found the broom and dustpan and swept up the broken bits of pottery. She knew he wanted her and clearly didn't understand why he was fighting it. With the low hum of arousal in his blood, he was trying to remember why himself. She'd said her piece back in the barn and now it was his turn to say...something.

Dumping the last of the shards into the trash, he pulled out the first aid kit to tend her cuts. She jolted a little as he took one delicate foot into his hands. His gaze flicked up to hers before coming back to his work. "I'm sorry."

He meant it as a blanket statement, but of course she didn't let him off that easily.

"For what exactly?"

His hands were a lot more competent at first aid for her injured foot than his brain was at spitting out actual words. "For hurting your feelings."

"My feelings aren't hurt." Despite her cool, matter-of-fact tone, he knew they were, at least a little.

Dousing a cotton ball in alcohol, he gently cleaned the wound. She hissed. He blew on the spot, trying to ease the sting, and Laurel went very still, her whole body tensing. But it wasn't pain he saw when he glanced up at her face. Awareness sharpened those long-lashed hazel eyes.

The woman valued honesty. He'd give her what he could. "It's not that I'm not attracted to you."

"Yeah, I figured that out. So what's the problem?"

Dabbing a bit of antibiotic cream on the cut, he fixed a bandaid over it. "It's just...you've got a lot on your plate. A lot of decisions facing you. Big, life-changing ones. It's not the right time to make that harder or muddle it with emotional complications."

"Nice try, making it all about me. But that's not why you pulled back."

No, it wasn't. He hadn't expected her to pick up on that. "You sound awfully confident for someone who doesn't know me."

"I'd like to."

Christ, don't hand me that temptation. I'm only so strong. "Laurel..."

"No really. I don't know what it is you think I'm looking for here. I do not have visions of forevers and white picket fences. It'll be years before I can even entertain the idea of that."

That had his head coming up to study her face. She believed it. Had clearly accepted this as her fate. But he could see the yearning underneath. She might not think she could have those forevers and white picket fences but, deep down, she wanted them.

"Why would it be years?"

"Freshly-graduated attorneys have no time for a life." The stiffness came back to her shoulders. "In six months, I'll be lucky to see the outside of my firm." At the last, her breath shortened. He could all but see the panic stalking her.

Not on my watch.

When he scooped her off the counter, her arms twined around him and she tucked her face against his throat. The show of vulnerability scraped away another layer of his defenses. Tightening his hold, he carried her into the living room and sank down on the sofa, cuddling her close, ignoring how good she felt tucked up against his body.

"Breathe."

"I'm sorry. I'm not doing this on purpose."

"I know." Sebastian stroked her back and murmured like he would to one of his horses, waiting until the tension bled out. "Why do you want to be an attorney?"

Settling her head against his shoulder, she sighed. "That's not a simple question."

"I've got time." Even if he didn't, he'd have made it for her.

"You know I'm a fair bit younger than Logan. I was the surprise baby. My parents thought they'd gotten what they wanted on the first go—a son who'd carry on the family name and follow in our father's footsteps. They loved me, but I was often a little of an afterthought. All the focus was on Logan. I adore my brother, but I was jealous, too. I kept wondering what I'd have to do for them to see me."

"Did you act out? Rebel?"

Laurel snorted. "About as far from that as I could get. Has Logan ever told you about the whole debacle of grad school for him?"

"Just that he studied psychology and decided in the long run that being a therapist wasn't a good fit for him."

"He was supposed to go to law school. That was The Plan for as far back as I can remember. Dad is, as you know, a lawyer, and our grandfather—Mom's dad—was a federal judge. When Logan went into psychology instead, Dad was disappointed. I think he'd always had visions of some kind of father-son firm. I was a senior in high school at the time, and I saw my chance. I was smart and competitive and I actually liked the law, so I decided I'd take a pre-law track and do everything he'd expected Logan to do. I had the grades and the academic chops to pull it off, and I was determined to earn his attention. I know that sounds pitiful."

If only she knew what he'd done in the name of earning attention. "No. I think it's natural to want our parents to be proud of us. We're wired to want that."

"Well, Logan apparently short-circuited that wiring because he bailed on grad school entirely. He was done with his Master's coursework and had been accepted to a PhD program. All he had left was defending his thesis. Our parents were furious. I think they'd have been furious either way because we were taught from a very early age that you finish what you start, and he walked away without ever defending. But the fact that he chose to become a farmer—that just killed my Dad. He came from humble beginnings, and he always wanted more. He worked his ass off, and he got it. The idea that Logan would choose something he considers lesser is, as you've observed, a massive bone of contention."

It would probably be rude of him to point out that her dad

sounded like a snobby, entitled douchebag. "Yeah, I got a sense of that."

"So right in the middle of all that, I announced I intended to pursue the law. Part of it was hoping to take some of the heat off Logan and part was because…I wanted to be the golden child for once. And I was. Dad noticed, and he loved that I shared that interest with him. I loved the praise and attention. When I got into Vandy for law school, he was over-the-moon excited. So was I, to start. I loved the challenge. That sense of competition and drive took me a long way. But Vanderbilt is one of the best law schools in the country. I've had to push so fucking hard to keep in the top one percent of my class. Which…really, was fine. I don't mind hard work. But as it's getting closer and closer to the actual reality of getting out of law school and really *being* a lawyer, that's when the anxiety started to take hold. And it all came to a head when I got offered that position up in New York."

"Which is what, exactly?"

"It's with one of the top five firms in the nation. That I got interviewed at all was a huge honor, and that they offered me the job…it's essentially the pinnacle of my academic achievement. On the surface, it sounds amazing. Insane starting salary, a deal on a swank condo near the office. A gym and dry cleaners in the build-ing. Runners to pick up any food you could desire. It sounds like a lot of perks, right? But it's because you're basically selling your soul for eighty-hour work weeks and a shot at partner."

Equal parts impressed and appalled, Sebastian leaned back to look into her face. "You've done all this to earn your father's approval?"

Laurel winced. "Pretty much, yeah."

He understood exactly the kind of toll it took to push yourself to the limits in the name of pleasing someone else. "It's impressive as hell. *You're* impressive as hell. But this is your life, Laurel. If you really wanted this, wanted that life, that would be one thing. But it's obvious you don't. And you can't do this to yourself for someone else. That's a really terrible reason."

She stiffened, straightening to look at him. "I don't have a choice."

There was always a choice. But she didn't want to make it. Sebastian recognized she wasn't in a place where he could convince her to stand her ground and take a page from her brother's playbook, so he'd let it go. For now.

"So what exactly do you want while you're here?"

Frowning, she made a long, wary scan of his face. "I want to relax. I want to not think about next semester. I want to get back in the saddle again." She paused. "And I'd like to get you know you better. Whatever that might entail."

He'd started this conversation intending to explain as best he could why getting tangled up together was a bad idea. But she was standing at a crossroads in her life, still primed to go headlong down the wrong path. Saving her from herself felt like something that would help balance his personal scales, paying forward the kindness and compassion he'd received from her brother. And, he selfishly wanted to get to know her better, too. He wanted to give in to this attraction. To take what she was offering for this liminal time before they both went back to their normal lives.

So he brushed a stray lock of hair back from her face. "Okay."

Laurel frowned. "Okay?"

"I can handle all that." *What the hell. In for a penny...* "And I'd be lying if I said I didn't want to handle you."

Her pupils sprang wide and the pulse in her throat began to hammer. Sebastian indulged himself, stroking a thumb over that sensitive point, feeling it flutter against his touch. She didn't close the distance. He realized that he'd have to make the move this time. So he did, leaning in to close the scant space between them.

He meant for the kiss to be sweet. He really did. But at the first brush of their lips, the heat between them exploded. Her hands dove into his hair, gripping his head so she could angle for a deeper kiss, and damn, her taking what she wanted was hot as hell. Heart knocking against his ribs, he licked into her mouth, loving how she met him stroke for stroke. On a growl, he skimmed his palms beneath her sweatshirt, up her torso to cup her breasts. Laurel moaned, arching into his touch. He devoured her mouth and wondered how fast he could strip her naked and plunge into all that softness. Apparently entirely on board, Laurel tipped back, dragging him with her. All but drunk on the taste of her, he twisted to follow…and rolled right off the sofa.

He crashed to the floor with an *ooph*, cracking his head against the hardwood.

"Oh my God. Are you okay?"

Sebastian sucked in a breath. "Fine. I just had a little sanity knocked into me." He was about to take her with no finesse, no forethought, and more importantly, no condom, on her brother's living room couch. Shit.

"Please tell me you didn't just change your mind about all this."

No. He hadn't changed his mind. He wanted her more than he wanted his next breath. But he also wanted to help her make a better decision than he had. To do that, their relationship had to be about more than just sex on every available surface—as appealing as that thought was. He needed to be her friend, not just a holiday fling. And if he was honest—and damned, he'd better get used to that since Laurel demanded nothing less—it was also about protecting himself. The only thing worse than never having her would be to have her knowing he'd never get another chance at that kind of perfection. So he'd have to set himself some limits. But only some. He was human, after all.

"No. I'm going to want to get my mouth back on you at the earliest opportunity."

She blew out a breath. "Thank God."

"But—"

"I hate 'but.'"

He dragged himself into a sitting position. "We're going to

slow this down a little bit." Now that the fog of lust was starting to clear a bit, he could see the sense in that.

"Slow it down? You do remember we only have ten days, right?"

"We aren't going to spend all of them in bed."

Her gaze sharpened on his face as she neatly stacked the paperbacks he'd knocked off, back on the coffee table. "The corollary of that is that we're going to spend some of them in bed."

God, this woman. "I'm gonna go ahead and tell you that the lawyer speak, when you're looking all mussed from my hands, is hot as hell."

She flashed a wicked grin. "I have so much more where that came from. But you didn't answer my question."

"Pardon me, counselor." He scrubbed a hand over his face to hide his smile. "Yeah, I expect that's going to be a foregone conclusion at this point. But right now, you're going to find some boots."

"Boots?"

"Yeah. We're going for a ride."

"It's so beautiful here." From the back of her mount, a sweet-tempered mare named Blossom, Laurel tried to look at everything at once. Her brother's land stretched far as the eye could see, with pastures giving way to cultivated fields. Even in the early winter, it made a picture. One that was rapidly imprinting on her heart. "I can see why Logan fell in love with it."

"He picked a helluva a spot, that's for sure."

"I can't even remember the last time I was really out in nature for an extended period of time. Maybe right after Logan bought the place, when I came out to visit for a week that summer. But that was before he turned it into all this. Before I started law school." And that was a dim, distant memory, buried under

56

hundreds of hours of lectures and thousands of pages of reading. "You know, it's lowering to admit, but this is the first thing I've done for pure pleasure in years."

"When was the last time you were in the saddle?"

"Oh man." She thought back. "High school." Horseback riding wasn't precisely like riding a bike, but she'd found her rhythm quicker than expected.

"Why is that? Did your parents make you quit?"

"No. Not overtly, anyway. I gave up riding when I started buckling down and getting serious about my future. I've been so driven and focused, always with my eye on the prize. I haven't taken the time just to breathe, to enjoy something for the sake of enjoying it, to get out in the actual world."

"And how does it feel?"

"Amazing." The ease and freedom were such a contrast to how she'd been living. It really brought home exactly how unbalanced her life was. Was that what had driven her brother to walk away from everything? She'd never asked him, maybe because she was afraid of the answer. But she could see the seduction of that kind of radical change.

Bo and Peep bounded ahead, pausing to sniff here and there before racing off again with cheerful barks. Sebastian rode abreast of her on a big, dark brown gelding named Brego, looking perfectly in his element. Still, even though they were in motion. How the hell did he manage that kind of Zen? Was it the land? The horses? Some combination of both?

"I'm really envying you right now."

One dark brow winged up as Sebastian glanced over at her. "Why?"

"To get a chance to do this all the time. That sounds like paradise."

His eyes crinkled at the edges. "It's not all trail rides all the time. Running a stable, even a small one like this, is a lot of work."

"You call sixteen horses small?"

"Well, I grew up on a farm with closer to a hundred, so yeah."

Laurel couldn't even imagine the true scope of that kind of operation. Whoever his mother had worked for had some very serious money. "My inner tween girl just had a major squee. What was it like?"

"Pretty fucking awesome. I mean…work. Always work. There was basically never a chance to sleep in, which sucked a lot in high school. And I have shoveled a lot of shit in my lifetime. But the horses…they were always worth it. Getting to see them run. Or better—being on their back when they did. There's nothing like it."

"No. No, there's not." She grinned at him. "Race you."

Before he could answer, she kicked Blossom into a canter, suffering a few bone-jarring strides before she found her seat. Sebastian and Brego caught them fast, but they stayed neck-and-neck as they raced across the pasture, toward the edge of the valley. The wind whipped her hair and stung her cheeks, and she felt more alive than she had in years.

By the time they eased their mounts back, she was laughing with unfettered delight. "That. Was. *Awesome!*"

"You've got a pretty good seat for someone who hasn't ridden in the better part of a decade."

"Are you checking out my ass, Sebastian?"

"It's an excellent specimen of God's artwork." Taking the lead, he headed for a trail between the trees.

They rode in silence for a while, slowly making their way up the mountain, with the dogs trailing behind, all canine smiles and wags. It was easy to be silent with Sebastian. There was no pressure or expectation for conversation. He was a man who only spoke when he had something to say. Laurel liked that about him. It made their conversations seem more important.

"Careful of the switchback. That fork there is more dangerous, with more difficult footing," he warned.

"Got it. What's up there anyway?"

"Way on further up, there's a ramshackle bootlegger's place. Hasn't been used in years, probably because the trail collapsed. But there's a cabin. It's not much to see, though."

Something about the idea that moonshine had been run out of these hills delighted her. "Really? How'd you know it was there?"

"I was in the area for a search-and-rescue training exercise and stumbled across it."

"You do search and rescue?"

"Stone County doesn't have a paid SAR team, so it relies on volunteers. I've got a certain skillset that's useful there, so it seemed like the thing to do."

And his hero points were just racking up. "You were military."

He grunted in acknowledgement. "Rangers."

Her interest sharpened. "You were Special Forces?"

"75th Ranger Regiment. Eight years."

"So, like, jumping out of planes and stuff?"

"Among other things." There was a wealth of possibility in those simple words.

"Wow. That must have taken an amazing amount of work."

"It did. I liked the challenge."

She could respect that. "Why did you get out? Why not career military after all that?"

He released an audible breath. "The challenge was no longer adding value to my life."

That set her back in her saddle. She'd spent most of her life chasing one challenge after another because she thrived on them. But had she ever given any thought to what value those challenges added to her life? The attainment of the goals at the end of those challenges, sure. But the value of the challenges themselves? She'd been so busy throwing herself whole-heartedly into them, the idea of questioning what she got out of it never occurred to her.

Not quite sure what she thought about that, she kept the focus on Sebastian. "Do you miss it?"

The silence stretched out so long, she didn't think he'd answer.

"The brotherhood, the purpose. Yeah. The job itself, no." The air between them was weighted with the things he didn't say about what he'd seen. The things he'd probably done.

His tone didn't leave the door open for more questions, so she lapsed into silence. Blossom was content to follow Brego, so Laurel let her have her head. The evergreens got thicker as they climbed, muffling the sound of the wind and blocking all view of the farm. It was easy to imagine they were alone, in the middle of nowhere. With that certain set of skills, Sebastian was exactly the kind of guy she'd want to have with her in that eventuality.

Her mind turned over what he'd said. She understood the need for a purpose, that desire to feel useful. His military skills had little place in civilian life, and it seemed in the absence of the Army, he'd fallen back on the skills he'd been raised with. Maybe there was a way to help him turn that into something more formalized.

"So you grew up around Thoroughbreds. Are racehorses where your passion is?"

"No. Not particularly. I love riding, and since I started working for your brother, I've remembered how much I love training. But I'm not competitive. Not with these horses, anyway. I find it far more gratifying to work with rescues to overcome abuse or neglect."

"That's very noble of you."

"Nothing noble about it. They saved me, so it only seems fair that I return the favor."

"I have a hard time imagining you needing saving from anything. You're always so in control and sure of yourself."

"I wasn't always." He dropped into another of those silences she wasn't sure she should interrupt. "Horses are prey animals, so they're extremely sensitive to their environment. They tend to mirror whatever mood or behavior they see from us. When I first started working with them again, the stuff they reflected back showed me I was volatile. Angry. I had a switch, and it took very little to flip it. To get anywhere with them, I had to earn their trust, and to do that, I had to turn that switch into a dial and learn how to turn it down so I could focus on them and what they needed. When I managed that—really managed it—I found the stillness I needed."

She wanted to learn how to do that. To be able to draw on that stillness in herself rather than always seeking it out from him. Because he wouldn't always be there. But that was a question for later. He was usually so reticent, and she wanted to keep him talking about himself as long as she could.

"So now you pay it forward."

"As much as I can, yeah. It's tough, though. Not being able to save them all."

"There are more?"

"Always. But even if we weren't out of space, the riding school, such as it is, doesn't pay enough to cover any more than we already have. It's a helluva thing having to turn any animal away."

No, he wouldn't be able to do that. He couldn't walk away from any creature in need—be they two-legged or four. That kind of compassion was beyond appealing. So was he.

Laurel opened her mouth to say so, but just then, they emerged from the trees at the top of a ridge and the view struck her momentarily speechless.

The whole world seemed to stretch out beneath them. From here, she could see the two branches of mountain that wrapped like arms around the tiny valley that encompassed Maxwell Organics. Other than the house and outbuildings, and a few other houses far distant, there were no signs of civilization. If she had her directions right, the town of Eden's Ridge ought to be on the other side of the ridge to the west. But none of it interrupted the magnificent view. In this moment, it felt like they were the only two people in the world.

"I needed this," Laurel murmured. "God, I had no idea how much I needed this." Her soul simply sighed. "Going back to

Nashville, to law school, to the never-ending grind is going to kill me."

"You made the choice to step on that path. You can make the choice to step off it."

That was reductivist thinking at its finest. But it was a lie. She'd been lying to herself. She thought she'd been in charge, in control of her life. But everything she'd done had really been reactionary, driven by her father's approval or disapproval.

"I don't know how," she whispered. "The idea of taking a leap off that road, into the unknown, is just as terrifying to me as staying on it. I mean, at least as an attorney, I have a plan. I know what's coming. And it feeds the challenge I crave. If I don't have that...then I have nothing. A wasted education. Wasted talents. A wasted brain." Not to mention her father would probably disown her. "I was raised to believe that I have a duty to serve the gifts I was given. And regardless of whether I agree with my dad on the nature of my career, I do believe in that. So until or unless I figure out some other way to serve those gifts, I can't see doing something else."

Sebastian stayed silent a moment as they both stared out over the valley. "Did you ever stop to think that maybe you won't be able to see that other way until you take everything else away from the equation?"

She couldn't even fathom it. "That feels like the height of irresponsibility. Logan had a plan when he dropped out of grad school. He knew he wanted to do this, and he's made it work. I've been focused on law my entire adult life. I don't have the first clue what else I'd do. In the middle of the worst of the panic and anxiety, I've tried to imagine it, and my brain just comes up with static. A total blank."

"The middle of an anxiety attack is probably not the best time to be considering your career alternatives. Either way, you don't have to know yet. You don't have to do anything but focus on the right now. Stop thinking about stuff that hasn't happened yet.

Regardless of what your dad wants, you haven't accepted that job. You haven't graduated yet. That decision is still out there. It's not set in stone. So focus on what's in front of you. For the next ten days, nothing else matters."

He was what was in front of her. And maybe he wasn't her future, but he was a helluva lot more appealing to think about.

"Okay."

"Okay?"

"I can handle that." Lips curving, she tossed his own words back at him. "And I'd be lying if I said I didn't want to handle you."

Sebastian threw back his head and laughed. "All in good time."

CHAPTER 6

"*L*unch or groceries first?" Sebastian asked.

Laurel's stomach chose that moment to growl. "I believe the jury has spoken."

"Lunch it is." He whipped into the first vacant space he found on Main Street. "The diner's a couple blocks up."

"I don't mind the walk."

Slipping out of the truck, they fell into step, shoulder-to-shoulder. Because he itched to thread his fingers with hers, Sebastian shoved his hands into his coat pockets. He didn't need to get used to easy, date-like behavior with her. This thing between them was time-limited. Plus, small towns were gossip central. No matter how much confidence Laurel had that Logan wouldn't bat an eye at their involvement, Sebastian would just as soon word of them being cozied up together didn't get back to him.

Eden's Ridge was decked out for Christmas, with pre-lit wreaths on all the street lights and a banner stretching across Main Street announcing some Christmas Bazaar the following week. Store windows were all holidayed up, with spray-on snow frosting the glass and a whole range of Christmas trees, reindeer, and Santas, in all manner of setups, reminding everybody of the season.

Laurel's smile seemed to grow wider with every store they passed. "Okay, this town is seriously cute. All it needs is a blanket of snow and it would be the perfect setting for a Hallmark Christmas movie."

Sebastian hadn't given a lot of thought to Eden's Ridge since he'd moved here. When he'd separated from the Army, he'd come to see Porter for some R and R, and stayed for the job. The town itself hadn't played much role in his decision. In truth, he didn't need to leave the farm for much, other than stopping by the feed and farm supply. With all the produce and meat produced by Maxwell Organics, he rarely even had to come into town for groceries. Logan couldn't afford to pay him much of a salary, but the trade-off of a roof over his head and most of the food he ate more than made up for it. His expenses beyond that were minimal. Sebastian wasn't a social guy and didn't have a clue what kind of stuff there was to do. Though, since Harrison and Ty had relocated here, too, Porter usually managed to drag them all out for a beer and a meal a couple times a month.

It was fun to see everything through Laurel's eyes. She tried to look everywhere at once, her step bouncing with excitement as they strolled. She stopped to admire some blown glass...thing in the front window of Moonbeams and Sweet Dreams, the florist and gift shop. "Oh, this is lovely."

Sebastian didn't have any idea what it was, but he supposed the vivid colors, bleeding one into the next, were pretty.

"I'll have to come back to do my Christmas shopping."

"I figured you were the type to have an itemized list that was all checked off by Halloween."

Laurel laughed. "You would be wrong. If it didn't have a grade attached to it, I haven't thought about it in years. I actually have picked up a couple of gifts already, but when I left Nashville, I hadn't planned on staying until Christmas. I need to get on that."

"Isn't that what Amazon's two-day shipping is for?"

She narrowed her eyes. "Are you one of those people who waits until practically Christmas Eve to do your shopping?"

He didn't want to admit he just didn't have many people to buy for, so it wasn't an issue. "Are you kidding? That would require I people. I'm not getting out in that madness. C'mon. I'm starving." Taking hold of her elbow, he steered her toward the diner.

Crystal's was the perfect, old-school, greasy spoon, with a black and white checkerboard floor and a lot of chrome and worn vinyl. The scent of grease and onions hit Sebastian as soon as he walked in the door and his own belly gave a grizzly bear growl. The place was packed with the lingering after-church crowd. Laurel moved ahead of him, making a beeline for the last remaining booth. She slid in on the far side, close to the kitchen—the seat he wanted, so he could see the door. He hesitated, debating whether to sit beside her for the best tactical position or take the opposite side and feel his skin crawl the entire meal, every time the door opened.

Cozy it is.

"Scoot over."

Surprised pleasure flickered over Laurel's face, when he slid in next to her. He realized his mistake almost instantly. These booths weren't big, not for a guy his size. Sharing one side meant they were pressed together from shoulder to knee. Awareness prickled his skin as she shifted, tucking an arm through his and tipping her head to his shoulder in a sort of mini-hug. It felt damned good to have her there, all snugged up against him, but the closeness was wreaking havoc on his good intentions.

He nodded toward the condiment stand. "Grab a menu."

Laurel leaned forward, her hand slipping down his arm to rest on his leg. She left it there as she held the menu where they could both see, commenting the various options that sounded good. Sebastian didn't hear a word because the warmth of her hand on his thigh had him mentally reciting past Kentucky Derby winners to keep from embarrassing himself in public.

"Well, well, well. Fancy meeting you here."

Just fucking perfect.

Ty stood at the edge of their table, deputy's hat in hand, his lips twitching into a smile, as he took in their cozy position. His sharp blue gaze dropped to where Laurel's hand rested on Sebastian's leg and the smile morphed into a full-out grin as he drew God knew what conclusions. "Are you gonna introduce me to your lady friend?"

No matter how much Sebastian wanted to shoot off an eat-shit-and-die glare, he couldn't say a damned thing. Because this was the first real sign he'd seen of the man Ty used to be, and he didn't want to shut his friend down. No matter what kind of hell he was about to catch.

As the silence stretched on too long, Laurel smoothly unwound her arm and looked to Sebastian for cues, but he could feel the fresh tension where her thigh touched his.

Shit.

"This is Laurel Maxwell. Laurel, this is Ty Brooks, one of my friends from Army days."

"Nice to meet you, Ty." It was the well-trained debutante reaching across him to offer her hand.

"Maxwell. Like Maxwell Organics Maxwell?"

"Logan's my brother. I came up for his wedding this weekend, and I'm sticking around to dog-sit while he's on his honeymoon."

"Oh, so you're staying out at the farm, helping Sebastian out?" He went brows up in an expression that was probably supposed to be innocent.

"Dude, you're really gonna have to work on your interrogation skills," Sebastian told him.

The arrival of their waitress cut off Ty's retort. As she took their drink orders, Sebastian caught Ty's eye and switched to eyebrow speech. *Drop it.*

Fine. For now. But I expect details later.

Sebastian scowled. *You're such a girl.*

With a sound somewhere between a grunt and a laugh, Ty plunked his hat on his head. "Well, I best be getting back out there. I'm on duty. Y'all have a nice lunch. Laurel, it was good to meet you."

She lifted her hand in a wave.

Sebastian nodded. "Later, man."

They both watched as Ty zipped up his Sheriff's Department coat and stepped outside.

Laurel pursed her lips. "You're gonna be hearing about this later, aren't you?"

"Oh yeah."

She winced. "Sorry."

Wanting to put her back at ease, Sebastian mustered a smile. "It's nothing I can't manage."

Their waitress came back with their drinks, and took their lunch order. They both got the Sunday Special: fried chicken, mashed potatoes, and green beans.

As soon as she was gone, Laurel shifted in the seat, back against the wall, so she could face him. "So you and Ty were in the Army together?"

"Yeah." She was clearly waiting for more. He didn't want to talk about his own time in the Army. But he knew he needed to give her something. "He's the last of our group to get out. Got injured from a roadside bomb and decided not to go back." That had more to do with losing his best friend to that IED than his own injuries, but that wasn't his story to tell.

"And now he's a deputy here?"

He nodded, sipping at his sweet tea. "Just started a couple months back."

"Did you ever think of switching over to law enforcement?"

"Not my thing. It'd require dealing with people, and I'd rather not."

She huffed a laugh. "You aren't doing so bad with me."

"You're not people."

The arrival of their food provided a natural break to the conversation, and when he steered things away from his service for the rest of the meal, she didn't pursue it. They continued to stick to easier topics as they walked the three blocks back to Garden of Eden for groceries.

Sebastian grabbed a buggy. "You can't be serious."

"As a heart attack."

"You seriously like *Elvis?*"

"Come on now. I'm from *Memphis*. It's practically a requirement for residency."

"Tell me you've at least picked up some better musical taste since you moved to Nashville," he begged.

"Such as?"

"I don't know. You're living in the country music capital of the world. You've gotta be appreciating some of that."

"I do have a soft spot for Garth Brooks and Trisha Yearwood," she admitted.

Sebastian mimed wiping his brow. "Oh, good. We can still be friends."

"Sebastian!"

The familiar female voice had his hands fisting on the handle of the shopping cart. *Of course.* "I'm sorry," he muttered.

Laurel only had time to widen her eyes before they were set upon.

"You've been hiding." Ivy swooped in for a hug.

Sebastian squeezed her back, relieved to see she wasn't alone. "Of course, I have. You keep using me for manual labor when I don't."

"It was *one time!* Okay, maybe two, but we're moved in now." She turned to Laurel, her eyes dancing with interest. "And who is this?"

Knowing Harrison's girlfriend would read more into an evasion, he didn't even try to get out of introductions.

"Ivy, Harrison, this is Laurel Maxwell. Laurel, my friends, Ivy Blake and Harrison Wilkes."

Everybody shook hands.

"Maxwell. Are you—" Harrison began.

"Logan's sister. Yes," she finished. "Does everybody know everybody around here?"

"Well, we've only been here a few months, but yeah, that's the general consensus," Harrison acknowledged.

Ivy threaded her arm through Harrison's. "Laurel, you'll have to come to dinner."

The out-of-the-blue invitation ruffled Laurel's usual social grace. "I...um..."

Harrison's lips quirked. "Way to segue, babe."

"Call it a consequence of constantly hanging out with all your friends. I'm starved for female company."

"Sure, we'll call it that," he teased.

Sebastian still couldn't get used to seeing his usually serious friend this relaxed. Love had made him soft, but in a good way. Ivy smoothed out his rough edges.

"Tomorrow night," she continued.

"No, you've got that conference call with your publicist," Harrison reminded her.

"Wednesday, then. You'll still be here Wednesday night?"

"Yes. I'm dog-sitting for my brother while he's on his honeymoon."

"So you've got a couple of weeks." Ivy exchanged a Look with Harrison, and Sebastian knew she was thinking sometimes that was all it took. For a thriller writer, she'd gotten all romantic and shit since she and Harrison got together. She'd been on a less-than-subtle crusade to play matchmaker. He needed to nip this whole thing in the bud. Laurel wasn't moving to Eden's Ridge permanently, so nothing could happen beyond this fling.

Maybe if he kept reminding himself of that, the idea would stick.

"She's not gonna take no for an answer," Harrison warned. "You might as well give in now. I know this from experience."

Ivy stuck her tongue out. "You love my dogged determination."

While they made googly eyes at each other, Sebastian scrambled, trying to find some means of getting Laurel out of this. But her expression was one of amused curiosity rather than annoyance.

"I'm sorry, I have to be a little nosy here...publicist?"

Ivy waved a hand. "Oh yeah, it's just a meeting to talk about further promotion for my latest book."

Laurel's eyes sharpened. "You're an author?"

"They both are," Sebastian added.

"What do y'all write?"

Ivy's grin turned impish. "Come to dinner and find out."

LAUREL GLARED at Sebastian in the driver's seat. "You're seriously not even going to give me a single clue?"

He only smiled. "Nope."

"Come on! Google failed me. There's not a single Ivy Blake or Harrison Wilkes listed on Amazon, so obviously they write under pen names. Won't you even give me a hint about genre?"

"Oh no, it'll be a lot more fun to watch you find out on your own."

On a huff, Laurel crossed her arms. She hoped her teasing snit would cover the nerves bubbling over this dinner. How the hell was she supposed to act tonight? It had been obvious what Ivy thought was going on when she'd issued the invitation. But Laurel wasn't Sebastian's girlfriend. They weren't dating. She didn't know exactly what they were because, despite their frank conversation to the contrary, he hadn't done more than kiss her.

Wonderful, addictive, toe-curling kisses, yes. But still, just kissing. It wasn't what she'd expected. He wasn't what she'd expected.

He'd put her to work the past few days. She had offered, of course, but she hadn't imagined he'd let her get quite so involved. While he'd been running lessons and working with some of the more problematic rescues, she'd mucked, groomed, polished tack, and ridden. He'd even let her work with a couple of his rescues that were further along, teaching her how to look past her expectations and read their body language and behavior. She'd had the time of her life, even if she'd been feeling aches in muscles she'd forgotten she had. If his master plan was to keep her too busy to dwell on the subject of what came next in her life, mission accomplished. It was probably just as well he hadn't tried to take her to bed yet. Every night, she fell into a virtual coma as soon as her head hit the pillow. Which was, admittedly, later than planned because of the side research project she'd started.

Sebastian stayed quiet the rest of the drive. He'd been pensive today, and she wasn't sure why. Was he dreading this dinner as much as she was? Or was something else going on? Had he realized he didn't want to pursue things with her and was trying to figure out a way to let her down gently? That was a depressing thought. She wanted him more than she'd ever wanted anyone. The idea that it could be one-sided made her want to shrink into the seat.

You don't have enough evidence to prove your case. Stop drawing unfounded conclusions.

"Laurel?"

The rumble of his voice pulled her out of her thoughts. "What?"

"We're here."

The generous post-and-beam cabin was lit up like a golden jewel against the winter dark. It was as warm and welcoming as its hostess, who threw open the door and waved them inside, her smile almost as bright as the house.

Laurel unlatched her seatbelt and started to climb out of the truck, but Sebastian caught her hand. "You okay?"

"Fine." She almost left it at that but couldn't resist adding, "Are you?"

His eyes widened a fraction. Then his expression softened and he squeezed her hand. "It's nothing to do with us."

Us. That one tiny syllable put her mind at ease.

Her shoulders relaxed. "Then let's go be social."

"Come in! Come in!" Ivy gave Laurel's shoulders a squeeze as she stepped into the entryway.

It should've been awkward. They didn't know each other. But Laurel found it impossible to hold on to her discomfort in the face of Ivy's genuine enthusiasm.

She half expected Sebastian to freeze up a little, as he had when they went to town. But he was far easier around Harrison and Ivy. It was clear, as they all worked to finish setting the table and prepping drinks, that the two men had a long history. And Sebastian treated Ivy with the same kind of fond, platonic teasing Xander had always directed at Laurel. By the time they sat down with food, she had relaxed into the flow of banter between good friends.

"So how exactly did you and Harrison meet?" she asked.

"Oh, well, I drove off a mountain because of a bear. Harrison is the one who rescued me."

Laurel's mouth dropped open. "Off a mountain?"

"I mean, it wasn't awesome—my Blazer was totalled—but it could have been a lot worse. And I certainly didn't cry about being trapped with all that big sexy for days because of a Tennessee blizzard." She waved her fork at Harrison. "Talk about inspiration. Which was good, since that was the whole reason I was running away to the mountains in the first place. I had the worst case of writer's block of my career."

"Do you write romance?"

Ivy's pale green eyes lit. "Sebastian didn't tell you?"

Laurel shot him another glare. "He said it would be more fun to see me guess."

She drummed her fingers together with glee and beamed at Sebastian. "You do love me!"

"Not my secret to tell, and I know how much fun you have seeing how long it takes people to get it."

"You've got to at least give her some clues," Harrison put in. "Fair's fair."

Ivy angled her head, considering. "Okay. It's not generally what people expect."

"You call that a clue?" Sebastian asked.

"I think Laurel can work with it."

"I do like a challenge." Setting her fork aside, Laurel studied her hosts. "I'm guessing Harrison was a Ranger. He carries himself like Sebastian does. If that was your inspiration, I'd narrow what you write down to romance or some kind of suspense. You said it's not what people expect, so that would lead me away from romance and more firmly into thriller or suspense. The kind of stories about a guy who can handle himself."

Her hostess grinned. "Getting warm."

"You mentioned a publicist the other day. I'm guessing they don't hand those out like candy, so that would seem to indicate a certain level of success."

"Warmer still."

"I haven't had much time to read for pleasure the last few years, but I did do some browsing of the best seller lists before we came over. I don't remember seeing many women among the suspense and thriller set. Which makes me think you might be pulling a George Eliot and using a male pseudonym. Or at least one that's gender neutral."

She mentally flipped through the names she remembered. One, in particular, had stood out with multiple entries that had stayed on the *New York Times* Best Seller list for months. Sitting across from Ivy now, a lightbulb went off. "Holy shit, you're Blake Iverson."

Ivy bowed with a flourish. "At your service."

Sebastian stared. "You managed to get to that from 'It's not what people expect?'"

"It's deductive reasoning."

"Dear God, now we have two of them," Harrison groaned.

"Don't worry, baby." Ivy patted his hand. "I'm sure it'll take at least until dessert for us to take over the world."

Sebastian still looked a little shell-shocked. "I'm beginning to see how it is you're at the top of your class."

Laurel grinned and shifted her attention to Harrison. "Now you. Your name wasn't anywhere on Amazon either, so also a pseudonym I'm guessing."

He angled his head in acknowledgement.

"Your former occupation would lend itself well to thrillers or suspense, but I'm guessing you maybe went in a different direction." She took in the Battlestar Galactica T-shirt stretched across his broad shoulders. "Maybe military science fiction?"

Amusement had his lips curving. "Keep going."

"I'm way less familiar with that as a genre, so that's about as far as I can go. Except…" She'd seen some military sci-fi in her brother's living room. That wasn't his usual genre. It stood to reason that maybe he'd check it out if somebody he knew actually wrote it. What was the name on the spine? She closed her eyes, trying to bring it into her mind.

Richards. Ramsey. Rawls.

"Russell. John Patrick Russell."

Ivy whooped and Harrison's mouth fell open. He glanced at Sebastian. "You told her."

"Hand to God, I didn't."

Harrison squinted at Laurel in suspicion. "Are you psychic?"

"No. Just observant. And very, very good at research."

"What is it you actually do?" Harrison asked.

"I'm finishing up my last year of law school at Vanderbilt."

"Yeah? What's your track?" Ivy asked.

"Corporate law." It was a natural enough question, but Laurel instantly began looking for ways to shift the conversation before it barreled on toward what came after school.

Ivy studied her. "It's not what you want to do."

Laurel glanced at Sebastian, who was frowning.

"No, Sebastian didn't tell me that. The moment I asked, you froze up. It's not what you want to do, but you've spent so much time on this path, you don't know how to do something else, and it's starting to freak you out because graduation is just around the corner. You've spent years defining yourself by your academic achievements, and you're about to be out in the real world, where you'll have to define yourself some other way, and you don't know what way that's going to be. You've got a good brain that you don't want to waste and, I'm guessing, a healthy sense of caution about switching to something else without having a solid plan in place. Not to mention, you feel like walking away from all the hard work of your education would be both a waste and a betrayal, and if you do that, what does that make you?"

Speechless, it was Laurel's turn to stare.

Harrison sighed. "Honey, we've talked about this. You're not supposed to profile the guests."

Ivy had the grace to look chagrined. "Sorry, sorry. Old habits. It's just, I get it. I know exactly what it feels like to struggle with that because I did it. I didn't start out planning to be a writer."

"What were you going to do?"

"I thought I'd be a profiler for the Behavioral Analysis Unit of the FBI. I've been profiling people most of my life, and I've got a graduate degree in forensic psychology. But I figured out that I didn't have the stomach for the real deal."

"So you just...switched to writing?" Laurel couldn't fathom making that kind of leap.

"Oh, that makes it sound like I had a plan. I totally didn't. But I was lucky enough to fall into the writing before I graduated, and it turned out that's what I was made to do."

"Do you regret having spent all that time on your graduate studies?"

"Not at all. My graduate training is part of why I'm good at my chosen genre. It's not at *all* what anybody gets a degree in forensic psychology for, but I've made it work. And the fact is…you can do all kinds of stuff with a law degree that doesn't involve business contracts or court battles. It may not be the most obvious path, but it doesn't mean whatever you figure out is the wrong one."

Laurel sat with that for a minute. All this time, her big example for changing directions had been Logan, who'd picked something totally different from what he'd been doing before. But Ivy, it seemed, was a lot more like her. Someone academically gifted, who'd finished what she started and found a non-traditional way to use the same skills doing something else. A something else at which she'd been monstrously successful. It gave Laurel hope that maybe there was an answer to her conundrum. One that would make her happy and keep her from being excommunicated from the family.

"It's certainly something to consider."

Ivy smiled. "And the middle of a dinner party with relative strangers isn't where you want to do it. I'll stop now." She shifted her attention to Sebastian. "Your turn."

SEBASTIAN HELD UP A HAND. Ivy's skills were always fascinating until they got turned on you. "I do not need my head shrunk, Ivy."

"No, but something's stuck in your craw," Harrison said. "And I'm guessing it's got something to do with that wellness check Ty took this morning."

"Wellness check?" Laurel asked.

Sebastian blew out a breath, wishing he'd come up with some

kind of solution. "Yeah. The Sheriff's Department got a call to do a wellness check out in the county. Older guy. Widower. He usually shows up at the feed and farm supply every couple of weeks to buy supplies for his chickens and horse. He didn't show this week, so Stan—he's the guy who runs the farm supply place—called to ask for a wellness check. Turns out Mr. Massey died. Several days ago based on—well, the evidence, as it were. The animals were starving."

Laurel covered her mouth. "Oh my God. That's terrible. What will happen to them? Did he have any family?"

"No. It was just him. A neighbor's gonna take the chickens, but there's nobody to take the horse. Ty saw that he got fed and watered and his stall cleaned out, but he needs a new home."

Understanding softened her expression. "And you can't afford to take on any more of them."

"What if we sponsor him?" Harrison asked. "We can afford to take on the cost."

An odd mix of embarrassment and gratitude swirled in his chest. That they'd offer was a mark of their long friendship, but that they had to... Sebastian had had enough of being a charity case. "I appreciate that, man, but it still doesn't alleviate the problem of space. We're simply out of room."

Laurel's expression turned thoughtful. "Can you rig up something for the short-term?"

"Depending on what he needs, probably. Why?" He could practically see the wheels turning in her head.

"Your primary issue with expanding the setup you've already got is funding. You said yourself the riding school barely supports the care of the sixteen horses you have. But what if you had other sources of income? The kind of income that would allow you to build bigger facilities, to house more animals, so you can keep doing the rescue work you love."

Why don't you wish for a lottery win while you're at it?

"It's a nice pipe dream, Laurel, but unless you've suddenly developed the Midas touch, I don't see how that's feasible."

"It is if you switch your focus to equine assisted therapy. You said yourself the horses saved you. This would give you the chance to offer others that same opportunity. And in doing so, it would open the doors for you to continue the rescue work you're really passionate about."

Sebastian was more than a little horrified at the idea. He already wasn't keen on being a riding instructor, and now she wanted him to become a therapist?

Apparently he didn't do a good enough job hiding his reaction because Laurel was leaning forward with that convince-the-jury gleam in her eyes. "I know you don't want to people. Just hear me out. You want the horses to be self-sustaining. There's not sufficient demand for a riding school in a place the size of Eden's Ridge to ever support the level of rescue you'd like to do."

The matter-of-fact way she cut down the one idea he'd had for bringing in money had him wanting to hunch his shoulders. But she was still going.

"Equine assisted therapy fills an established need. I know I don't have to cite the statistics on homelessness, substance abuse, and suicide among veterans to you. Those are the men and women you served with. Friends. There's considerable research documenting the efficacy of equine assisted therapy as a treatment for everything from anxiety to depression to PTSD and more. I'm proposing that you establish a therapy program that expands what you have now to hire an equine therapist, who'd do more of the peopling. Logan would probably have some ideas on that front. We can talk to him when they get back, but either way, that would free you up to do more of the animal rescue and rehab you love, and would bring in more money overall to support the program and possibly expand in the future."

"Oh, that's *brilliant*," Ivy said.

It was pretty brilliant. She'd come up with a solution that took

KAIT NOLAN

into account everything he'd told her. How he wanted to make the horses self-sustaining so they—and he—were no longer a drain on her brother. How he wanted to spend less time with the people and more with the horses. He'd read some about this type of therapy and knew it was a thing. Given his own experiences with horses, he had no trouble believing it worked. But it was so huge, so much of an undertaking, and she still hadn't addressed the matter of funding.

"I still don't understand where the money would come from."

"Grants. There are 60,000 nonprofits in North America that account for more than seven billion dollars in funding from federal, private, self-help, and therapy programs for veterans. There's all kinds of funding out there. All you have to do is find and apply for it."

That sounded about like searching for a needle in a haystack. "You just fill out an application and they'd hand over money for me to build another barn or whatever?"

"Well, it's a bit more complicated than that. Different grants have different stipulations. But the biggest hurdle for most people acquiring that kind of funding is the actual grant application. They're usually needlessly complex and overwhelming. It so happens you have someone on your side who's an expert at navigating the needlessly complex and overwhelming. I've already got a stack of half a dozen options printed and annotated back at the farm."

Sebastian only stared at her.

In the Army, he'd been the problem solver. The guy everybody else came to for help. He never asked for help himself, even when he needed it. It was a pattern that had continued even after he got out. He'd been wrestling all damned day with how he could help this horse. Hell, he'd been wrestling for weeks about how he could expand the program, period. And she'd offered a solution.

He had no idea if something like this was really possible. No idea what Logan would think or if it had a chance in hell of working out. But in this moment, he was incredibly moved by the fact that she'd put so much caring thought into a problem he'd mentioned to her without asking for help, and that she'd come up with something that really took the things he'd said into consideration.

Beside him, Laurel's excitement dimmed. "It was just a cursory search. If you'd rather focus on the equine rescue side of things, I'm sure there's something out there. I can—"

He held up a hand, cutting off the rest of whatever she was about to babble. "Stop."

Folding her hands in her lap, she slipped on that polite mask he'd seen her wear around her parents. "I'm sorry if I overstepped. I'm sort of conditioned to research and document. It's an occupational hazard."

Sebastian just shook his head, trying to line up his thoughts to set her back at ease. "It's not that."

"What is it then?"

"I'm accepting reality."

Frowning, she leaned toward him. "You don't have to give up. We can figure something out. I'm sure there's—"

"Not about the horse."

How the hell was he supposed to defend against this woman? With her big brain and even bigger heart? As a Ranger he was trained never to admit defeat. To keep going. Keep pushing, come hell or high water. But strong and stubborn as he was, he didn't think he could keep fighting against what he felt for her. He wasn't even sure he still wanted to.

"I'm talking about the fact that I'm completely, unavoidably crazy about you."

Sebastian imagined it took a helluva lot to make Laurel Maxwell speechless. He wanted to lean over and kiss that stunned "Oh" right off her lips.

Across the table, Ivy gave a squee. "I knew it!"

"Shut up, Ivy." He reached out and found Laurel's hand

beneath the table, uncurling her clenched fingers and lacing them with his. "Thank you. I don't know if the grant thing will work or not. We'll talk to Logan about it when he gets back. But thank you for trying, either way."

A pleased blush spread across her cheeks and down her throat. "It seemed like the least I could do."

"Your least is more than a lot of people's most. You're a helluva woman."

At the sound of a shutter click, they both looked over to Harrison, who had his phone in hand.

"What the hell are you doing?" Sebastian demanded.

"Documenting. Ty and Porter would never believe it otherwise."

"You're a dead man, Wilkes."

Harrison only grinned. "It's totally your turn."

CHAPTER 7

*L*aurel stayed quiet on the drive back to the farm, her brain too full to flirt. For the first time in maybe ever, she actually felt like there might be a way out of the cage she'd backed her way into. Ivy was right. There were more options with a law degree than the ones she'd been chasing. She'd just never explored them because they weren't part of The Plan, and The Plan had been writ in stone practically since time immemorial.

As Sebastian parked his truck by the barn, he braced an arm on the steering wheel and turned toward her. "You okay?"

"I'm just thinking about what Ivy said."

"Ivy said a lot of things tonight."

His dry tone had Laurel huffing a laugh. "Yeah, she did. I like her. She was stunningly correct in her profile of me. It's so hard for me to even conceive of doing something else because it feels like giving up. Because when you're gifted at anything—academics, the arts, whatever—that's how your stewardship over your own gifts is presented—over and over. If you don't use them, it's a waste. It's something that's always been important to me, so I've never let myself think about doing anything else."

"Are you thinking about it now?"

"Hard not to. Which is scary as hell."

"Change often is. Come up to the house with me. I want to tell you a story."

They slipped out of the truck and he took her hand for the walk up the hill to his little cabin. She loved the feel of his broad, work-roughened palm against hers. That blend of strength and gentleness in those hands were so representative of the man himself. The one who'd admitted he was crazy about her. The knowledge made her giddy, and she hoped that meant she'd be feeling those hands on the rest of her before the night was through.

"You asked me the other day why I didn't stay in the Army after becoming a Ranger. That wasn't the right question. The question is why I went into the Army in the first place."

"As much as you love horses, I wondered."

"I never knew my father. He wasn't ever involved and Mama married Kevin when I was about three, so I don't remember anybody else. He was the one who raised me. When he was around, anyway. He was career military, gone on deployments a lot of the time, so most of the actual parenting was done by my mom and Walter."

"Who's Walter?"

"Walter Perkins. He was the head trainer and something of a surrogate father to me when Kevin was away. " He unlocked the door and let them inside, heading straight for the coffeepot. "Make yourself at home."

Laurel shut the door and paused. The house was barely a thousand square feet, with an open-floor-plan living room and kitchen, and a short hall that led to what were probably a couple of bedrooms and a bath. The furniture was minimalist, with a La-Z-Boy recliner and what had to be a second-hand sofa clustered around a coffee table made of reclaimed wood. Other than some kind of horse magazines loosely stacked on the table, there were no knicknacks, no pictures, nothing that showed personalization or permanence. Because he was just that minimalist or because he didn't let himself believe he'd get to stay anywhere?

"Sorry for the bachelor chic decorating. I don't exactly bring people up here, and I don't need much for just me."

Conscious that he might feel embarrassed because of what she came from, Laurel grinned. "Are you kidding? I nabbed my grand-daddy's La-Z-Boy for my first apartment. I love that chair. It's perfectly broken in and has hosted many a nap." She crossed over to lean against the island, wanting to get him talking again. "Get back to your story."

Sebastian methodically measured out coffee grounds and added water to the machine. When it began to gurgle, he kicked back against the counter opposite her, curling his hands tight around the edge in an uncharacteristic show of agitation.

"A few weeks before I graduated high school, Mama and Walter went to deliver a horse that'd been sold. On the way back, they were hit by a drunk driver. My mother was killed on impact, and Walter died in the ambulance." She saw the quick slash of pain rip through him, even as he tried to mask it.

Horrified, hurting for the boy he'd been, Laurel pushed away from the island, crossing over to wrap her arms around him. "I'm so sorry, Sebastian."

For a moment he only stood there, wooden. She could only imagine the fear and anguish he was remembering. At last, he bent, pulling her closer and burying his face in her hair. They stood that way, in silence, until the coffeemaker beeped. Even then, he was slow to release her.

"Kevin was deployed at the time. It took him more than a week to make it back to the States."

Alone. He'd been alone through all of it. The idea of it had a knot of tears forming in the back of Laurel's throat, but she held them in as he kissed her brow and turned to pour the coffee.

"After the funeral, he didn't know what to do with me. And why should he? He'd been gone more than he was home. But we were all each other had left. There was no money for college, even if I'd been interested in that. The people Mama had worked for offered me a job, but I couldn't see staying there without her or Walter. It hurt too damned bad. So when Kevin suggested I consider enlisting, I did."

She couldn't even imagine it. Going to boot camp with that loss still raw and no support at all.

"It finally gave us something in common. And I got it into my head that if I made it to the Rangers, became the best of the best, that he'd be proud of me. I didn't see or hear from him a lot during those months. He was deployed and I was working my ass off. When I graduated Ranger school and got assigned to my battalion in the 75th, I managed to set up a video chat to tell him. Know what he said?"

Laurel accepted the mug he offered. "What?"

"'Good for you. That makes you a grown-ass man who can take care of yourself now. Watch your six and have a good life.'"

The man was supposed to have been Sebastian's father. His family. And he'd just written him off? Laurel couldn't fathom it. Outraged, she set the coffee down with a thunk. "Have a good *life?* What the hell was wrong with him?"

Sebastian cupped his own mug between his palms. "I thought it was the grief talking. So I applied myself to the job with the same dedication I'd given to the training. I figured I'd work my way up the ranks, and then he'd see. I was good at it, and I ended up in a unit with Harrison and Ty. I found a second family. That part was good. But Kevin...it took me years to accept that he never actually thought of me as his son. And at that point, I realized I'd been doing all this shit for the Army, not because I believed in it, but in a vain attempt to impress somebody who was never going to be impressed. So I got out."

To do that much work, put in that much effort, doing what was arguably one of the hardest jobs in the world, only to realize it was all for naught. Laurel couldn't imagine it. But she was starting to see where he was going with this story.

"And then you came here?"

"Not at first. I spent about eighteen months drifting. Working odd jobs. Trying to get a handle on my shit. All the stuff that I did in the name of duty—a duty I didn't actually feel that bone-deep call to do—that really fucked with my head. It had some serious consequences for me, trauma I'm still dealing with. Stuff I expect I'll always be dealing with. But I'm telling you all of this to illustrate the futility of living to please someone else. The real crime, as it relates to you, isn't in using your gifts on a different, less obvious path, but in using them to serve somebody else's ideal, in a life that isn't going to satisfy you. And that's why I keep pushing you about this. Because I don't want that for you."

His pivot made it clear that he was done talking about himself. He wasn't looking for comfort or sympathy. This had all been about illustrating his point, so she did what he wanted, shifting mental gears back to her own situation.

"I don't want that for me either."

"What do you want?"

He'd asked her that so many times since she'd come to Eden's Ridge. Each time, fear had held her back from really considering the question. But tonight…tonight she felt like she finally had an answer. Or part of one, at least.

"I'm not sure. But it's not just that I don't want the job in New York. I don't want to be a lawyer. I don't want to be what my father wants me to be." She blew out another breath and felt like her next inhale was freer, easier. "God, I really mean it. I don't want to be a lawyer." It was a huge thing to admit. To him. To herself. Because it meant finding a new path, a new plan.

"It's not too late to change. I did. And maybe I'm still figuring out what that new life looks like, but I made the choice. You just took the first step. How's it feel?"

She considered the question. Considered, too, the man who'd

pushed her past her fear to get to this point. She wouldn't have gotten here without him.

"Like a weight's been lifted. It's scary and exciting. And...it feels like something worth celebrating."

~

As she looked up at him through lowered lashes, Sebastian's blood began to heat.

He'd held off and held back, wanting to earn her trust, to convince her she could and should do something other than what she'd been working toward.

Mission accomplished.

But that hadn't been the only reason he'd held back. He'd thought he could keep a part of himself separate. That he could stay emotionally uninvolved, so that when she left, it wouldn't hurt. But she'd blown that all to hell tonight, with her grand plan and her unquestioning faith that he could pull it off. No matter what, it was going to cut him off at the knees when she walked away. So he'd take what she offered, give them what they'd both wanted from the start.

Very deliberately, he set his coffee aside and slipped her mug from her fingers. "That definitely feels like something worth celebrating."

He slid his palms along hers, absorbing her shiver as he folded his fingers around her slim, delicate hands. "You know, I told myself I wasn't going to do this. I was going to maintain some boundaries."

A flicker of irritation clouded her expression. "For my own good?"

He shook his head, gaze steady on her face. "For mine. I don't let myself get attached to people, and I don't do meaningless encounters. I knew from the beginning that being with you could never be meaningless. You aren't a one-night fling sort of woman."

One dark brow winged up. "What am I then?"

His thumbs traced circles on the insides of her wrists, feeling her pulse jump. "You're a fight-all-the-dragons-in-her-name-and-take-her-home-to-Mom kind of woman. And one night or one week will never be enough."

"Oh." She was an incredibly articulate woman, always ready with a comeback, and Sebastian found great satisfaction in reducing her to monosyllabic shock for a second time in one night.

"I told myself it would be worse if I let myself have you and knew what I'd be missing when you go. But hell if I can walk away from you. So if you don't want this…If you aren't absolutely sure, you're the one who's gonna have to step back."

The shadow in her eyes faded as she stepped forward, closing the distance between them. "I want this. I want you."

On a groan, he closed his lips over hers, swallowing her sigh. He was already hard as he drew her in, pulling her tight against him. She shifted to rub her hips against the bulge in his jeans and opened for a deeper kiss, sliding her tongue against his. The taste of her flooded into him, sweet and sinful, leaving him dizzy and desperate for more.

He needed skin. Needed to feel the warmth of her in his hands, against his tongue. Tunneling beneath her sweater, he released the catch of her bra and filled his palms with her breasts. They were heavy and perfect, the nipples already drawn tight with desire as he circled them with his thumbs.

"Oh, God." Her eyes blurred and she sagged a little as he traced each taut peak. "More. Definitely more."

On board with that, Sebastian stripped off the sweater and bra, baring her chest to his hungry eyes. Her creamy skin was flushed, the dusky rose of her areolas giving way to deeper pink nipples.

"Gorgeous." Bending, he took one tight bud into his mouth.

Laurel whimpered, pressing closer as he licked and sucked, each pull making her rock her hips against his, and driving him just a little more crazy. Skating his hands down her spine, he slid them into her pants, thanking God for leggings as he slid them and her underwear past the curve of her hips. Releasing her nipple with a light scrape of his teeth, he knelt, sliding off her short boots and easing the fabric down the rest of the way.

Her breath went ragged as he helped her step free. Seeing her there, unabashedly naked in his kitchen, her eyes full of lust and longing, had his dick going impossibly harder. He ached with the need to lift her onto the nearest horizontal surface and drive himself into her. But that would be over too quickly. He wanted to draw this out. Make it last.

"Such soft skin." Sebastian skimmed his fingers from her ankles up the backs of her legs, thinking of all the ways he wanted to worship her beautiful body. But he could already scent her arousal, and that overrode everything else. "I'm going to kiss every inch. But right now, I need to taste you. Hold on to the counter."

"Oh."

Again with the monosyllables. It made him smile. But when she didn't move, he looked up to find her eyes closed, her expression strained.

"Laurel?"

Her eyes snapped back to his, pupils swallowing up almost all the color of her eyes. "What?"

"You okay with this?"

She ran her fingers through his hair, lightly scraping her nails over his scalp in a way that had him leaning into her touch. "I am very okay with this." With one, last, nipping kiss, she leaned back and gripped the counter.

Sebastian kept his eyes on hers as he shouldered her legs apart, making sure she was still with him as he kissed his way up the sensitive skin of her inner thighs. She trembled and swallowed. Nerves, not fear. Satisfied she was okay, he spread her folds and licked. Her hips bucked against his mouth and she moaned.

"So fucking sweet." Leaning closer he hooked his hands behind her thighs and set to work, seeing to her pleasure with the kind of ruthless, single-minded focus he gave to a mission.

Her hands came away from the counter, threading in his hair as he drove her wild.

"More," she gasped. "Please, more. I need...I need..."

Sebastian slid two fingers inside her as he circled her clit with his tongue and she broke, flying over that first brutal peak screaming his name.

Her legs trembled as he lifted his head and shot her a cocky grin. "I never imagined you were a screamer."

Sagging back against the counter she stared down at him with heavy-lidded eyes. "Neither did I."

Rising, he skimmed his hands up the back of her legs, over her ass. "That was pretty much the hottest fucking thing ever. I want to hear you do it again, when I'm inside you."

Another shudder ran through her as she hooked a hand around his nape. "Then hurry up."

Sebastian boosted her up, wrapping her legs around his waist and kissing her as he strode with purpose to the bedroom. He lowered her to the bed, pulling away only long enough to break land speed records striping out of his clothes and grabbing a condom from the bedside table.

"Hurry." Her word was a chant in his blood as he stretched out over her and settled in the cradle of her hips, his erection just brushing her entrance.

"Hurry."

She was drenched and ready. He'd seen to that. He could slide inside her in one hard, fast thrust, and drive them into oblivion. But as he ranged over her, looking into the face illuminated by light spilling in from the hall, he paused, wanting to etch the moment into memory. This brilliant, beautiful woman wanted him. Needed him.

And he needed her.

The truth of it washed over Sebastian and left him reeling. This was more, so much more than what he'd intended.

She cupped his jaw. "Sebastian."

He saw his own vulnerability mirrored in her eyes and lost some of the frenzy. So he didn't hurry. Lacing his fingers with hers, he fixed his gaze on her face as he slowly flexed into her, one slow millimeter at a time. He drank in every nuance of her expression as he filled her. The friction was an exquisite torture, and his body trembled with the effort to maintain control.

When he was buried to the root in her tight, wet heat, he dropped his brow to hers. "Fuck, you're perfect."

Her body clamped around him as she arched up, tightening her legs around his waist, and his eyes all but rolled back in his head.

"You feel so good."

Sebastian kissed her again and began to move, taking everything she gave of her body and more, until they were both gasping, and she was begging. *Harder. Faster. More. More. More.*

And as her orgasm struck her like a blow and the hard clench of her body dragged him over behind her, he knew when it came to this woman, he'd always have the same demand.

More.

CHAPTER 8

"Well, the bank or executor or whatever is gonna have their work cut out for them." Sebastian stood beside Laurel as they both took in the sprawling farmhouse with the peeling paint and warped porch steps. The whole thing had an air of sad neglect that probably spoke to the age and infirmity of Josiah Massey. He didn't want to think about what he was going to find in the larger-than-expected barn about fifty yards from the house. Not that it mattered. The property wasn't his problem. His only concern was the horse.

Hunching her shoulders against the cold, Laurel shoved her hands into her pockets and continued to study the house. "Oh, I don't know. The place has good bones. It could be really cute with a fresh coat of paint and some window box planters. Maybe a porch swing. It just needs some TLC."

Amused, Sebastian glanced over. He knew Laurel well enough by now to understand that, despite her upbringing, she wasn't snobbish in the least. But her attitude still surprised him. "I wouldn't have expected you to be into the idea of a fixer-upper."

She shrugged. "I appreciate a house that's really a home, not a showpiece. The house I grew up in was featured in architectural magazines. God forbid we leave shoes by the back door or our beds unmade. What would people think?" She tipped her head back to take in the expanse of the house, and Sebastian could practically see her assessing, making lists of what needed to be done. "A place like this looks lived in. Like you could kick your feet up on the porch rail and relax with a glass of lemonade or a mug of hot coffee. It's why I've loved visiting Logan's farm. There I can relax and just *be.* Hanging out with the dogs, walking around in sock feet and ancient jeans and my most comfortable sweater."

That was the real Laurel, Sebastian realized. The one who didn't need artifice or social graces or worry about appearances. The one who'd shared his bed last night as if she'd always been there.

When she headed toward the house, Sebastian found himself following.

Climbing the porch steps, she stroked a hand along one handrail. "If this were my house, I'd paint it a lovely blue gray—you know that color you see in the Blue Ridge Mountains—with a nice, crisp, white trim. I'd get those big hanging ferns for all along the front. Maybe a couple of half whiskey barrel planters to flank the front door, filled with petunias or impatiens. Something really bright and cheerful. The barn would be painted red."

Willing to play along for a few more minutes, he nodded. "Naturally."

"I'd hang a porch swing just here. An oversized one that had room for cushions. Or maybe one of those old fashioned two-person gliders like my grandparents had. And every morning, I'd come out here so I could drink my coffee and watch the horses." She leaned against the porch rail and sighed in contentment, as if she could actually see the view.

Coming up behind her, he caged her in against the rail, loving when she leaned back against him. "There are horses in this fantasy?"

"Obviously. I mean, look at the size of that barn." They both glanced toward the massive structure that had clearly housed far more than a single horse at some point in the distant past. "What else would I use it for?"

"What, indeed?"

As she continued to paint a picture with her words, Sebastian could see it. He could see her here. More, he could see himself here beside her. He could imagine waking up with her, as he had this morning, rolling over to make sleepy love to her before starting his day with barn chores and coffee and the fuel of her sweet, sweet smile. He liked having her in his bed, in his life.

And that was a dangerous thought. No matter what else she decided to do for her career, it wouldn't be sticking around in tiny town Tennessee to be with him. She wanted to use that big, beautiful brain of hers, and there was no need for it here. At the end of this trip, she'd be going back to Nashville, and from there to who knew where. They had an expiration date. He'd do well to remember that.

Needing to get away from the mental image she'd created before it burrowed in and made a permanent home in his head, he straightened, and headed for the truck.

By the time Laurel joined him, he'd dropped the trailer ramp and grabbed a lead rope. "Let's go meet Maestro."

Morning light filtered in through high windows, illuminating the long aisle down the middle of the barn. It was bigger than the one at Logan's place, with more than two dozen stalls at a glance.

"Big place." Laurel's voice echoed in the empty space.

"Yep. It's old, but well-built. Looks like he or whoever came before him had quite the operation at one time." Curiosity stirred. At a little over two thousand people, Eden's Ridge wasn't big enough to justify a place like this just for boarding horses. A facility this size had to have been used for breeding or training. Tennessee Walkers? Quarter Horses?

"I wonder why Mr. Massey was down to the one horse."

"Couldn't keep up with more than the one I guess."

At the head of the row, a hoof gave a sharp rap against a stall wall.

"Impatient," Sebastian murmured.

"I don't blame him. Didn't you say he'd been on his own for several days until yesterday? I'm surprised Ty got him back into the stall."

"Yeah. I want to get him out, look him over for any injuries. Ty's not experienced enough to notice anything that's not major. There's a good chance he might've hurt himself trying to get out when he got hungry enough."

At the stall door, Sebastian got his first look at Maestro. At a solid sixteen hands, the Appaloosa was a dark gray, stretching back into a spotted white that was characteristic of the breed. Or he probably was under the dirt. "Well aren't you a big, beautiful bastard?"

The gelding snorted in irritation, tossing his head as if to say *What took you so long?*

Sebastian fished one of the carrots out of his coat and held it out on the flat of his palm. Maestro neatly plucked it up, inhaling it in three, quick bites before shaking his head and turning a restless circle.

"You like that, huh? How about another?"

They went through the routine twice more before Maestro tolerated a stroke down the nose.

"Let's get you out and see what's what." Carefully, Sebastian unlatched the stall door and eased it open.

Something darted past his feet with a yowl.

Laurel jumped and screamed. "What the hell was that?"

They both stared at the pile of hay where the creature had disappeared. "Not sure."

Her cheeks paled. "Rats don't make that kind of a noise, do they?"

"No. At a guess, I'd say a cat. I guess our boy hasn't been here all alone after all." Turning back to the stall, Sebastian slipped inside, automatically latching it behind him as he turned to wait for the gelding to come to him.

It didn't take long. He let Maestro sniff, stroking down the strong neck. This horse definitely hadn't been neglected beyond the past few days. He wasn't skittish or ill-tempered. It was a refreshing change to what he usually faced with a rescue.

"Open the door for me, will you?" Clipping a lead rope onto Maestro's halter, Sebastian led him out of the stall and out into the brisk winter sunshine.

In the corral, he tied the gelding to a rail and carefully ran his hands over every inch, checking for heat or other signs of injury or infection. Maestro tolerated the inspection, shifting occasionally and swishing his tail, but otherwise minding his manners.

"He's in good shape. Could use a good grooming, but otherwise, he's no worse for wear."

"What will happen to him?"

"I'll take him for now. But after that...it'll depend on what happens with Massey's estate. From what Ty said, there was no next of kin to inherit. I don't know what was in the old guy's will, or even if there was a will, but I expect the property will be sold to pay off any debts against it. The horse might be considered part of that. Depends on what the executor says, I guess. We'll see he's taken care of in the meantime."

Laurel stroked the horse's neck. "Then let's load him up and take him home."

Hearing her call the farm home gave Sebastian another moment of pause. A tiny flicker of hope began to flare that maybe...just maybe...

Don't be a fool.

He understood the parameters of this thing between them, and forevers weren't a part of it. The sooner he got that through his thick skull, the better.

Clucking, he tugged his new charge toward the trailer.

At the ramp, Maestro balked. "Come on now, bud. You can't

stay here." Sebastian circled him around and tried again with the same result.

"We've got company," Laurel said in a low voice.

Sebastian glanced back to see a scruffy gray tabby cat bellying out of the barn. The animal was missing most of one ear and had a scar beside its left eye that gave the thing a piratical look. Maestro bobbed his head and the cat rose from its crouch to prowl a few steps closer.

"Guess they were barn buddies," Sebastian said.

"We can't just leave him here." Laurel crossed toward the cat, dropping into a crouch when the thing flattened against the ground. "Come here kitty. Come here baby."

Sebastian had his doubts about whether they'd actually be able to catch the tomcat. "Let me load up Maestro, then I'll help you round up the cat."

This time, when he led the horse to the trailer, he clopped right on up the ramp. "Good boy."

Once the horse was secure, Sebastian went to help Laurel, bracing himself for the prospect of claws. As he stepped out of the trailer he stopped dead at the sight of her with a massive armful of cat. The big tom had a purr like a rusty motorboat, his green eyes slitting with pleasure as she scratched behind his one good ear.

"Well, that was fast."

"This guy's just a big softie. Yes, you are." She cuddled up to the beast as if it were a tiny fluffball of a kitten instead of a clearly proven brawler.

"I think his scars indicate otherwise."

"So do yours, but you're a big marshmallow, too."

Sebastian's mouth dropped open.

Laurel only laughed and blew him a kiss. "I promise I won't tell your Ranger buddies and ruin your cred."

This woman had pegged him in a week. What the hell was he going to do when she left?

~

"Looking good, Trish. Okay, now I want you to try a trot. Sitting instead of posting this time."

Laurel followed the sound of Sebastian's voice out to the training ring, where a blonde in a bright blue parka sat astride Blossom. Her considerable breasts bounced with every step. Laurel winced in sympathy as Sebastian called out instructions for how Trish could fix her seat. Still watching the pair circle, he crossed over to meet her at the rail.

"Not a lot of natural aptitude with this one," Laurel murmured.

"Everybody's gotta start somewhere." He raised his voice. "Take two more laps, then drop back to a walk and start cooling Blossom down."

"Oka..a..ay." Trish bounced through the word.

As Sebastian turned to her, Laurel hauled herself up on the bottom rail so she could catch his mouth in a quick kiss. She didn't miss the instant scowl on Trish's face, and hid a smile. The woman wasn't here for the horses.

Sorry, honey, this one's mine.

"Do you have any more lessons today?"

"Not until later this afternoon. Why?"

"Because it occurred to me that the last thing Logan and Athena are gonna want to do when they get back is decorate for our parents. I want to run into town and get a Christmas tree, and maybe stop at the holiday bazaar."

"Sounds good. Let me just finish up here, and we'll head out." With another brush of his lips, he turned his attention back to his student. "Heels down, Trish!"

She'd just asked the man to go shopping, at a craft fair, and he hadn't uttered a single protest.

He just might be the perfect man. Phase one, complete.

That was the easy part of her plan. The next step had her squirming in the passenger seat of Sebastian's truck as they headed toward town a half hour later. He was a cautious guy. She needed the right words to sell him on this.

One corner of his mouth quirked. "Either I've popped a spring in my seat or you've got something to say. Spit it out."

Of course he could tell she had something on her mind. Because he could read her like a freaking book. She shifted to face him. "I've been doing some thinking."

His grin was easy. "You do a lot of that."

"I do, yeah." She took a bracing breath, still not knowing exactly what she was going to say, but aware she had to start somewhere. "Josiah Massey's property."

The grin faded. "What about it?"

"I know it's a little rough around the edges, but it would be ideal for either an equine rescue center or an equine therapy center, whichever you decided you wanted to do. It's not actually in too bad a shape."

His hands tightened on the steering wheel. "And you would know that how?"

Wincing, she hoped this didn't cross a line for him. "Ivy told me Porter is a contractor. I called and had him go out to do an evaluation of the structural integrity of the house and barn, and work up an estimate of both what it would take to bring it up to any kind of code, and what it would take to make it shine. He emailed the report back this morning."

When Sebastian said nothing, she rushed on. "The place needs more work than I'd hoped, but it's not outside the realm of possible. I was right that both the house and barn have good bones. There's still some question of what the property will go for, but there's not a lot of demand for a place like that in Stone County. The bank won't be able to offload it fast and would be likely to entertain lower offers just to get rid of it."

A faint ripple of something that might've been exasperation disturbed his blank expression. "You're talking about moving the entire operation away from Maxwell Organics."

"Yes. There's more space out there than you have at Logan's, and I'm sure he has his own plans for what he wants to do at the farm. This would give you room to expand, would really mean you could make it yours."

He'd already taken ownership of the horses. This was the next logical step. But Sebastian seemed less enthused by that prospect than she expected. If she hadn't been watching him so closely, she might've missed the flicker of doubt.

He wasn't sure he could do it. All along, he'd been cautious about the idea. She'd thought that was entirely a matter of the money. But she realized he actually didn't know if he'd be able to pull off what she was proposing. What did she need to say to convince him of what she already knew—that he'd be amazing at this, if only he'd believe in himself?

He glanced over at her, softening his expression into something that was probably meant to let her down gently. "It's a big commitment. And at this point, it seems kind of cart-before-horse. There's still the matter of money. I don't have it."

"I've found some more grants."

Sebastian just nodded. "We'll talk about it with Logan, after the holidays. If we get the funding and the place is still available, then we'll see what's what. It doesn't make sense to plan for an entire organization and program around property I don't own."

Laurel had the power to make it happen. Or would in a few months. But she couldn't say that. It would be too much, too soon, and she'd probably already gone too far. So she settled back in her seat. "It was just a thought."

On the rest of the drive, she babbled about favorite Christmas movies, determined that this wouldn't become the white elephant between them.

Town was busy, with people strolling the sidewalks and cars lining both sides of Main Street.

"Seriously? How can you not have seen *Polar Express?*" she demanded.

"I was over the age of ten when it came out."

Laurel stuck her tongue out at him, pleased when he huffed a laugh. "Fine, then, Mr. Mature. What is *your* favorite Christmas movie?"

"That's easy. *Die Hard*."

"*Die Hard* is not a Christmas movie."

Sebastian wheeled the truck into a space about three blocks down from the VFW, where the bazaar was being held, and clapped a hand over his heart in dramatic fashion as he mimed being stabbed. "You did *not* just say that."

"I did."

"I don't know if I can be with a woman who doesn't like *Die Hard*."

"I never said I didn't like it. It's a fantastic action movie. But there is no Santa in a sleigh shouting 'Yippee ki yay, mother fucker', ergo it is not a Christmas movie."

His laugh boomed out, dissolving the last of her tension. "Would that make it better?"

"I mean, at least then it would qualify."

Still debating, they slid out of the truck and joined the throngs on the sidewalk. He wrapped an arm around her shoulders, pulling her into his side as they walked.

"What's going on today? Is the holiday bazaar that big a thing?"

"No idea." Sebastian craned his neck. "Looks like something's going on in the city park. There's a line for something."

At her first sight of the "something", Laurel squealed. "Oh my God! It's a llama-drawn sleigh!" A team of four llamas was hooked up to a painted plywood sleigh. Each one wore an elf hat over its long ears. A small sign toward the front of the line announced *Pictures $5*.

"This will never happen again. We have to get pictures!"

Sebastian was laughing as she dragged him to join the line.

"Well hey, y'all."

Laurel swung around to find Athena's sister, Kennedy, and

Xander approaching from the opposite direction. Ari was with them. As soon as the girl caught sight of her with Sebastian, she broke into a wide grin and did a little fist pump. Xander arched a brow at their joined hands.

Laurel just arched hers right back. She was a grown woman, capable of making her own choices, and he didn't get to go all big brother on her in Logan's absence. "Hey."

"Logan mentioned you were sticking around the farm." Kennedy's lips twitched. "I'm guessing that's going well."

"It's been a lot of fun. I'm doing a lot of riding."

Xander made a choking noise, and Kennedy popped his chest with the back of her hand. Laurel's cheeks heated. That *so* wasn't what she'd meant.

Sebastian directed the conversation to Ari, as if nobody had picked up on that double entendre. "She's been working with Ginger. The mare's coming along well. She might be ready for you to give her a try in the next couple of weeks."

"Really? That'd be awesome!"

Smart move. Distract the horse-crazy matchmaker.

Pru and Flynn joined them as Ari and Sebastian continued to talk horses.

"What's this now?" Flynn asked. "Hello, Sebastian. Laurel."

"Dad! I might get to ride Ginger in a couple of weeks!"

"Well now, that's something, to be sure."

Laurel held in a snicker at his non-answer. "Aren't you down a family member?"

Pru rubbed her hands together to warm them. "Oh, Maggie's babysitting to give us a chance to get out of the house."

Flynn folded both her hands in his, automatically warming them for her. "She's delighted for the chance to spoil the baby. Meanwhile, I'm delighted for a chance to spoil this one." He tugged his wife in for a kiss.

Pru beamed up at him. They were obviously besotted with each other.

They all continued to talk, inching forward in line. Laurel watched Athena's sisters with their husbands, noting the way Kennedy instinctively edged into Xander, how he toyed with the ends of her hair, always seeming to need that physical connection. Hearing the easy way Pru and Flynn finished each other's sentences. The five of them were obviously a tight-knit, happy family, content with the lives they'd built here.

"Next!"

Laurel startled, realizing it was their turn. Sebastian helped her into the sleigh. He dug out a five dollar bill as she handed the attendant her phone, with the camera app open. They snuggled together on the seat, heads bent.

"Say reindeer!"

"Reindeer!"

"Okay, one more." The attendant lifted the phone.

"There's mistletoe, y'all," Ari shouted.

Laurel glanced up to find that one of the other handlers was dangling a sprig over their heads from a fishing pole. Sebastian grinned. "Can't let that go to waste."

"It would be bad luck," she agreed, already tipping her mouth up to his.

His lips were soft against hers, the kind of kiss that spoke of patience and promise, and Laurel melted into him.

"Oh, that's a good one." The attendant's voice dragged her back before she could lose track of their surroundings.

She stepped out of the sleigh, accepting her phone and swiping open her photos as Kennedy and Xander piled in behind her.

Sebastian leaned in to look over her shoulder. "Those llamas look ridiculous. We look pretty good, though."

They looked more than pretty good. They looked...perfect. Happy. Happier than she'd looked in...maybe ever.

She glanced back at her sister-in-law's family, and realized that this was the challenge she wanted. The whole package. The town. The life. And the prospect of that kind of love. With Sebastian.

CHAPTER 9

From where she lay sprawled atop him on the sofa, Laurel stared at the freshly-decorated Frasier fir now occupying a prominent corner of the farmhouse living room. "We do good work."

Sebastian tunneled a hand under her sweater to stroke up and down her spine. Their time was almost up. In thirty-six hours, Logan and his new bride would be back from their honeymoon. Laurel would have to move back into the guest room instead of his bed. Her parents would be inbound the day after that. And then she'd be going back to her regularly scheduled life and whatever new direction she figured out. He wanted as much of her as he could get before then.

"It's a good lookin' tree. And I'm pretty sure not having to scramble to make everything presentable for your folks will secure you a spot in the favorite sister column."

"Here's hoping they like everything. I may have gone a little overboard at the holiday bazaar."

He laughed, remembering the slightly manic look in her eyes as she'd moved from booth to booth—woman on a mission.

"Maybe a little. You'd think you never saw handmade ornaments before."

"We didn't have that kind growing up."

"Really? No popsicle stick sleds or pasta angels? I think most of our tree was covered in the stuff Mom and I made when I was little."

Laurel snuggled closer, rubbing her cheek against his shoulder. "I'd have loved that. But no, we didn't have homemade or hand-made ornaments. That kind of thing would never have been allowed on one of Mom's trees."

"It wasn't a family affair?"

"Oh no. It had to look good for the Christmas cards, so she went with theme trees she either decorated herself or hired a professional to do."

That sounded...impersonal. "Theme trees?"

"Yeah. Like, one year we had this big beach vacation. She brought back shells, spray painted them gold, and hung them, along with a bunch of peach ornaments." She propped herself on his chest, expression dialed to righteous indignation. "Peach! Peach is not a Christmas color, Sebastian!"

From the floor, Bo and Peep both popped up, ears pricked, ready for action.

Sebastian's lips twitched as he tried not to laugh. "That sounds...uh—"

"Awful. The word you are looking for is awful. I mean, some years were better than others. The beach tree was the worst of the lot. But we never had the fun, homemade ornaments to pull out every year. The kind that tell a story. Because that didn't look good."

Digging his fingers into the tension in her back, he began to knead. "That seems to be a recurring theme in a lot of the stories you've told about growing up."

She grimaced. "Oh God, yes. So much of the life I was raised in was about appearances. I don't care about appearances. I care about what's real." Her eyes turned serious. Leaning up, she cupped his cheek, brushing a soft kiss against his lips. "My time here with you has been real. Maybe more real than anything I've felt in my life."

She really knew how to take his breath away. He felt the same, and something sharp twisted in his chest that she was already thinking about the end. He didn't want to talk about that. He didn't want to talk at all. Satisfied with the idea of seducing her as distraction for them both, he slid a hand into her hair.

"About the Massey farm."

Sebastian froze. He didn't want to talk about *that* either. "I thought we agreed to hold off on that discussion until after the holidays."

"I didn't actually agree to anything. I don't mean to pressure you, but I don't think you're really giving the idea the consideration it deserves."

Oh, he'd thought about it, and the whole idea made him uncomfortable. In typical Laurel fashion, she was thinking way too big. Too much. He was a realist. Once she went back to Nashville, he intended to research ways to make the rescue itself self-sustaining and stop worrying about the idea of moving it off-site.

Knowing how much time and effort she'd put into crafting a solution for him, he chose his words with care. "I'm not trying to dismiss the idea. I'm beyond flattered that you think this is something I'm capable of pulling off. But it's not that easy. A program of the scale you're describing would require a shit-ton of admin and paperwork and I don't even know what all kind of details. Maybe all that seems easy for you, because you deal in details, and all the legalities of running something like this are no big thing for you. But I'd be completely in over my head. And wasn't this supposed to be about me getting more time with the rescues?"

"That's why I'm proposing to do this with you."

"I know you've said you'll help with the grant applications—"

"Not just the grants. All of it. I want to do this with you."

Hope mule-kicked him in the chest. She couldn't mean that how it sounded. Could she?

Sebastian hardly dared to breathe. "What are you saying?"

"You're right. Details and legalities *are* easy for me. It just makes sense for me to stay and take that part over so you can focus on the part you love." She curled her hands into his shirt. "I know it's crazy and fast and too soon. But I've always been direct with you, and we don't have that much more time. You were right that a week isn't enough. I don't want to walk away."

Her words echoed through him like a mortar blast.

She wanted to stay. It was the thing he hadn't let himself wish for, hadn't even let himself think about. But this wasn't as simple as she was imagining. She had a romanticized view of things, and one of them had to keep a foot in reality.

"You shouldn't stay just for me. Just to handle all the crap I can't or don't want to."

"It's not just for you. As I've gotten more into researching this whole thing, the more I really want to do this, for myself. It's completely different from anything I'd considered before, but it would still use my skills, and I *like* that. Honestly, I don't know if it will ultimately be my thing, but it's something I know I can do. And, really, I love the idea of what we could accomplish with this. We could make a huge difference in a lot of lives."

This was her new challenge. She'd never be satisfied mucking out stalls and giving kids pony rides for longer than a few weeks. She needed more. But the more was so damned huge.

"You've been asking me for more than a week what it is I want, and I've finally figured that out. Or part of it, anyway. I want to follow my brother's example. To be brave. To choose a different life. To choose *more.* I want that more with you. I want to give us a chance."

Sebastian wanted that chance. He wanted it more than anything he'd ever wanted in his life. But to get it, he had to agree to taking this leap of going out on his own. Except, it wouldn't be on his own. Not with her in his corner. She was a formidable woman, one who he had no doubt could and would handle all the details that would surely come up. That made the entire prospect less terrifying.

He could see it. How they'd work together. How they'd be happy. How they could make a life together. And even though the idea of dreaming as big as she did was more terrifying than his first solo parajump, the idea of losing her scared him more. If this was really what she wanted to do—to build the therapy center, run it, staff it, chase the funding, all while leaving him to the business of rehabbing the horses—many, many more horses than he could serve now—that all sounded pretty amazing.

FOR A LONG TIME, he said nothing, his face inscrutable, his body tense. The longer the silence drew out, the harder Laurel's heart pounded. The anxiety she thought she'd banished since she'd been here began to curl through her, insidious as smoke.

I knew it. I knew this was too much, too fast.

Or maybe that wasn't it at all. Maybe he hated the idea. Worse, maybe this had been just a fling to him and he didn't even want her to stay. It didn't feel like that to her, but anything was possible.

Oh my God. Say something before my heart beats straight out of my chest.

"You really want to stay?" The question came out rusty with emotion.

Laurel jumped at the tell. "Yes. I want to stay. I want to help you set up this program expansion. I want the chance to see what we can be together."

One hand slid into her hair as his eyes searched her face, dark and intense. "I can't ask you to do that."

And she understood that he couldn't ask. Because he didn't let himself ask for anything. Asking opened him up to rejection, and that was a position he wasn't willing to take. But she was more than willing to close the distance.

She cupped his face. "You're not asking. I'm making the choice, Sebastian. To choose this life. To choose you. If you'll have me."

He loosed a shuddering breath and dropped the stoic mask, pressing his brow to hers. "Thank God. I didn't know how the hell I was going to let you go."

At the sight of all that raw need in his expression, her heart rolled over in her chest. "Then don't. Don't let me go." Tightening her grip, Laurel kissed him, sinking into the spiraling warmth of relief and wanting.

"Laurel." He said her name like a desperate prayer of thanks and tightened his arms around her, tugging her so close, she could feel his heart hammering against her chest. Only then did she understand that he'd been afraid. Afraid of losing her. Of not being enough. Knowing that she mattered, that she wasn't in this alone, she fell just a little bit deeper.

"Sebastian." She sighed it, melting against him, wanting to assuage that lingering fear. To show him that he was enough. That he was everything.

He pressed his face into the juncture of her neck and shoulder, as if he just needed to breathe her in. Tenderness welled up at that small sign of vulnerability. Threading her fingers through the short hair at his nape, she held him close, grateful—so grateful— that this wouldn't be the last time.

On a sigh, he brushed his lips along her throat in slow, nibbling kisses. Laurel hummed with pleasure and tipped her head to give him better access. He trailed his way along her jaw, igniting little fires as he went, until their mouths met and clung. His hands stroked down her spine to the backs of her thighs, urging her legs apart so she straddled him. The bulge of his erection pressed against her center and she rocked against him. Want kindled to need, until heat pooled low in her belly and she shoved up his shirt. He reared up to tug it off as she did the same.

"So beautiful," he rasped.

She felt beautiful when he looked at her like that, eyes gone almost black with desire. Reaching for him, she brought his hands to her breasts, loving the feel of his callused fingers on her flesh, cupping, kneading. She ignited at his touch, rolling her hips to grind against him as he circled her nipples with his thumbs. She would never get enough of that bold possession. Because she was his in every way that mattered.

"Need you. Need you so damned much," he murmured, his expression fierce.

She knew what it cost him to admit it. Because he didn't let himself need anyone. His life had been one lesson after another that people would leave him. But she wouldn't. Because she needed him just as much.

"Then take me."

They lost themselves in a frenzy of desperate hands and tongues. Touching. Stroking. Stripping away every remaining barrier, until she straddled him again and the tip of his cock nudged her entrance. Rolling her hips, she stroked him through her wetness, loving the erotic friction of his flesh against hers, desperate to feel the rise and fall of his body beneath hers. She wanted him inside her more than she wanted her next breath, but when she wrapped her hand around his erection to guide him home, his big hands gripped her hips, his expression twisting to one of borderline pain. "Wait."

"What's wrong?"

"Condom. Don't have one here."

They'd spent all their naked time at his house, where there was a ready supply. It had been the smart thing to do and an easy non-discussion. But he wasn't the only one that had them covered.

"Don't need one. I haven't been with anyone but you in two years, and I've got an IUD."

"I haven't been with anyone else since I got out of the Army. But are you sure?"

"I need you, Sebastian. Right now."

His fingers tightened on her. "I'm yours."

"Mine." Gaze locked on his, she sank down, taking him in, claiming him in one long, slow slide.

He filled her up, body and heart. This kind, beautiful man who was her port in the storm. As she rolled her hips, setting a torturous rhythm, she felt the words trembling on her tongue. Even in the midst of the heat they made together, she knew it was still too soon. They had time. So she swallowed back the declaration and rode him, until they'd both forgotten everything but the glide of bodies and the slide of skin against passion-slicked skin. And when she shot over the edge into bliss, his name on her lips, he gripped her hips and followed.

CHAPTER 10

*B*etween late nights with Laurel, early morning training sessions with his rescues, and the last pre-holiday riding lessons, Sebastian was one step above a riding zombie as he went through the motions of running Maestro through his paces. Muscle memory and long-ingrained habit were the only things getting him through at the moment. That and the fact that the gelding was already exceptionally well trained. Surefooted and responsive, he was a dream to ride. If he ended up staying, he'd make an excellent addition to the riding school. Or the therapy program. Because there was gonna be one of those now.

He still couldn't quite get over it. But Laurel was all in, throwing the full power of her determination behind planning. She'd already filled up a legal pad with notes on things to research and questions for her brother. Watching her do her thing was both intimidating and sexy as hell, and it was easy to believe everything would be fine simply because she willed it to be so.

But in the dark of night after she drifted off and in silence just before dawn, doubts nipped at him. What if she changed her mind? What if her plan didn't work? Was he making the wrong decision for the horses? Was he thinking with his dick right now?

Or was he thinking with his heart, which sure as hell wasn't any smarter?

Needing to see her, he throttled Maestro back to an easy walk and turned toward the barn. "Let's cool you down and get on back."

The newlyweds would be back today. Sebastian was nervous about seeing Logan again. Stupid, maybe. But no matter how much of a non-issue Laurel thought their involvement would be for him, it was a very different thing to be confronted with the reality. Logan knew better than many exactly what kinds of shit Sebastian had struggled with. Sebastian wouldn't blame him if he had concerns about their relationship.

As he and Maestro crested the rise, the training ring came into view. Easing his mount to a stop, Sebastian watched Laurel circle the edge on Gingersnap. The woman was a natural. After the initial couple of days, she'd remembered everything she'd forgotten about horses and had been an invaluable pair of extra hands. Since that first day, he'd sensed a bond growing between her and the chestnut mare. The proof of it was right in front of him as they worked. Ginger was more confident, more spirited than he'd ever seen her, and Laurel seemed in her element. Watching the two of them, he really felt like he could see her doing this work, being satisfied by it. Being satisfied with him.

That lingering disquiet faded. She'd be happy. Certainly happier than if she went back to school and wound up working eighty-hour weeks at some fancy-pants law firm. And he truly believed that she'd be the exception to his life experience. She would stay. Because Laurel Maxwell didn't make promises she didn't intend to keep.

In the stable yard, he took care of Maestro before turning him out in the pasture and wandering over to the training ring for a closer look. "Looking good."

As if suddenly wary of having an audience, Ginger took a few dancing steps before Laurel gently brought her back under control. "She knows I'm nervous."

"No reason to be nervous." Okay that wasn't strictly true, but he didn't want to see her anxiety start spiraling out of control again. She'd made so much progress over the past week.

Laurel shot him a Look and folded her hands over the pommel. "We both know that's not true."

Sebastian climbed through the rails and strode toward them. "I'll be right there with you. You don't have to confront your parents by yourself unless you want to."

"Much as I would appreciate the backup, breaking the news to them with you there will make them think I'm bailing on every-thing for you." She swung her leg over the saddle.

Though she didn't need it, he reached out a hand to steady her back on the way down, just because he wanted to touch her. "Aren't you, kind of?"

"I'm bailing for me. You're a massive side benefit." Rising to her toes she popped up to kiss him.

When she would have pulled away, he banded an arm around her waist, hauling her in for a better taste. In a quicksilver flash, sweet turned to heat. Sebastian groaned as her mouth opened readily under his. Maybe they could squeeze in a quickie in the tack room.

At the sound of tires on gravel, they both froze before springing apart like guilty teenagers. The horse blocked them from view, but Laurel took a big step back from him. "Quick, do I look like I've just been kissed?"

Color rode high in her cheeks and her lips were red and a little swollen. "Uh…"

"Damn it. Stall them." She ducked away and went to finish cooling off Ginger. Or maybe herself.

Not having a horse in hand himself to delay the inevitable, he scrubbed a palm over his face and slipped back through the rails, crossing to where Athena's car had parked by the house. She and

Logan spilled out, looking relaxed and happy, with a honeymoon glow he could see from twenty feet away.

Logan lifted his hand in a wave. "How are things?"

"Good."

"Any problems while we were away?"

"Nothing I'd call a problem."

"Uh, what is *that?*"

Sebastian followed Athena's gaze to where the rescued tom was curled at the edge of the porch, tail twitching with suspicion. "Oh, that's Mr. Rochester."

She went brows up. "Didn't realize you were a Jane Eyre fan."

"I'm not. Laurel is. She's the one who brought him home and named him. He came with the new horse."

"We got a new horse?" Logan asked. "Did we have room for another one?"

Sebastian rubbed the back of his neck. "Yeah, about that..."

Laurel bounded over. "You're home! Sorry, I had to finish cooling Ginger from her workout." She threw her arms around her brother.

Logan squeezed her back, lifting her clear off her feet before setting her down and holding her at arm's length, searching her face. "You look better. Really good, actually. I'd say time on the farm has been good for you."

"So very good." Would her brother recognize the sappy, happy smile for what it was?

Logan's gaze shifted to Sebastian. *Shit.* A rare bout of nerves began to dance in his belly. Logan had left Laurel in his care, not in his bed.

She stepped into the awkward silence with enthusiasm. "I got to ride nearly every day, and Sebastian's let me work on training with some of the horses that are further along. It's been amazing. And you won't believe it, but I actually read a book *for fun.* I haven't had time to do that since I started law school."

Logan held Sebastian's gaze a moment longer before turning back to his sister. "And you apparently acquired a cat?"

"Well we couldn't just leave him. He's Maestro's barn buddy."

"Maestro?"

"The new arrival," Sebastian explained. "We'll tell you all about him once you're settled."

Athena scowled. "Guh, there's no time to get settled. We still have to decorate. Why did we think it was a good idea to get married so close to Christmas and then *host*? I'm hoping I can sweet-talk my sisters into coming over to help. If we have the Reynolds army, it won't be so bad."

Laurel bit her lip. "Actually, we already decorated."

"You did?" Logan asked.

"Yeah. I didn't think you'd want to have to rush to do that when you got back. And I bought you a bunch of cool ornaments from the holiday bazaar as a wedding present. I mean, we could easily do more if you want, but the tree's up and there's greenery all over the place, so the basics are done—ooph!"

Athena yanked Laurel into a hard hug. "That is the best Christmas present you could give me. Your mother intimidates the hell out of me."

Laughing, Laurel squeezed her back. "Aren't you supposed to be a badass and all?"

"I am in most areas, but I'd just as soon not get off on the wrong foot from the very beginning with my new mother-in-law."

"Glad I could help. I know it's stressful being the ones to host Christmas, and I want this to be as...peaceful as it can be."

Logan eyed her. "That sounds ominous."

Sebastian waited, wondering if she was going to tell her brother she'd decided against being a lawyer. But Laurel just shrugged. "I'd like to avoid a repeat of your rehearsal dinner. Dad doesn't have a filter anymore, and he shouldn't pull that shit in your home."

He tweaked her ponytail. "You don't have to be the mediator, Pip."

"Someone has to."

The pause went on too long, belying the joking tone. This probably wasn't the time or place for the discussion that needed to happen, so Sebastian stepped in. "I expect y'all are tired and would like to go on in and get settled. Let us help you with your luggage."

Athena linked arms with Laurel. "You boys handle that. We're gonna talk menu."

Suddenly alone with Logan, Sebastian reached into the trunk. "So how was Oregon?"

He straightened, suitcase in hand, to find Logan studying him with that neutral therapist gaze. Somehow the total lack of judgment in his expression felt like an indictment. It took all Sebastian's training not to fidget or fill the silence.

"You're good for her. I knew you would be."

Wait, what?

His confusion must've showed because Logan laughed. "A blind man could see the connection between you at our wedding. I'm not blind. Glad my plan for nature to take its course worked out."

Sebastian stared. "You set us up?"

"Let's just say I facilitated."

"Why?"

"Because you see her. In the middle of that shitshow my dad pulled at the rehearsal dinner, you made sure she was okay. She puts up a good front, but she hasn't been okay for a really long time. You're the first thing in a decade to crack that mask and make her even think of slowing down. I figured if anybody could get through to her, it would be you. All signs point to me being right."

Uncomfortable with his astute observations, Sebastian rubbed the back of his neck. "You're really okay with me being involved with your baby sister?"

"You're one of the best men I know, and you look at her like she hung the moon. Why wouldn't I be?" Logan dragged the other suitcase out of the trunk. "C'mon. I figure my wife can be induced to make food. She's been missing her kitchen."

Laurel's parents were arriving any minute. Because she wanted to reach for the antacids in her purse, she headed out to the barn instead, hoping to find Sebastian. Her own chores had already been finished an hour ago, courtesy of the fact that she'd woken even before the rooster began to crow. The only reason she knew she'd slept at all was the stress nightmare she'd jerked out of in a cold sweat. First one in two weeks. Except instead of the usual nightmare about being literally caged at a high-powered law firm, this time she'd dreamed she told her parents her decision and been cut off from the family. Given the imminent possibility of that reality, she hadn't been able to do more than choke down coffee.

She found Sebastian in the tack room. Knowing Logan was up at the house, cleaning up, she walked straight into his arms, burying her face against his chest and burrowing in.

"Hey now. What's all this?" He cuddled her close, his familiar scent of leather and horse settling over her in a blanket of comfort.

"Missed you."

"You saw me this morning." She could hear the amusement in his tone.

"I missed you last night. Apparently, I can't sleep without you anymore."

"My bed did feel awfully empty." He tipped her chin up, searching her face. "Bad dreams?"

"Yeah." Through the little window past his shoulder, Laurel could just see her parents' car pulling up in front of the farmhouse. "They're here."

Sebastian brushed a soft kiss over her lips. "You've got this. And you've got me."

Laurel dredged up a smile. "That's getting me through all of this." Squaring her shoulders, she pulled on the armor that had been second nature most of her adult life, surprised to find it didn't fit as comfortably as it had two weeks ago. "Into the breach."

"Good luck."

At the tack room door she paused. "I know you have a lot of work probably, but if you want to pop in for snacks in a bit, Athena's put together a bunch of appetizers, and I think Logan's making cocktails."

Sebastian's smile spread slow and easy. "I was just finishing up. Let me go grab a shower, and I'll join y'all in a bit."

Pitifully relieved, she blew him a kiss and went to meet her parents.

Athena was already greeting them, giving Rosalind an awkward hug. "Logan will be down shortly. He's just getting cleaned up."

"Hey y'all!" Laurel called.

"There's my girl!" her father boomed, pulling her into a hug.

Laurel gave him a squeeze. "How was the drive? Y'all made good time."

"We did." Stepping back, he surveyed her from head to toe. "You look kind of a mess, don't you?"

Resisting the urge to smooth down her hair, Laurel fought not to grind her teeth. Since she hadn't planned on being here for two weeks when she packed, the jeans, sweater, and no makeup had been her uniform. "I've been on vacation, dad. The dogs and horses don't care how I look."

Rosalind pulled her in for a hug as well. "I think you look more relaxed and that the quiet time was good for you."

"It was, thanks."

"Well, I hope you didn't play the whole time. You won't get this kind of uninterrupted time to study for the bar when you get back to school for spring semester."

Laurel's stomach clutched. *God forbid I do something other than work my ass off.* "I'll find a way to juggle everything. I always have."

"That's my girl."

Praying for patience, she followed everyone inside.

Logan came down, hair still wet from the shower. There was another flurry of hugs and handshakes, then Athena none-too-subtly herded them out of the kitchen and into the living room.

Rosalind's gaze swept the space, lingering on the Frasier fir. "Oh, the tree really fits the whole country farmhouse aesthetic."

This time Laurel lost the fight to not grit her teeth.

Athena slid her arm around Logan's waist. "Thanks! We really love it."

Knowing the remark was really for her benefit, Laurel shot her sister-in-law a grateful smile.

Logan waded into the lull. "We weren't sure whether you stopped on the road or not, but Athena's made some appetizers, and I thought we could all do with some celebratory cocktails."

"That sounds lovely," Rosalind assured him.

Her brother took orders and Laurel helped Athena bring in the trays of canapés. As everyone settled in around the living room, conversation turned to Logan and Athena's honeymoon in Oregon. Sebastian came in at the tail end of a description of the amenities of the resort.

"Oh good, you made it." Logan flashed a grin. "You would not *believe* the stables of this place. They looked like something out of *Rich Horseman's Quarterly.*"

Sebastian plucked a slice of bruschetta off a tray. "Oh, I'd believe it. I saw plenty of that growing up in Kentucky. A lot of those horses live better than most people."

"You're from Kentucky?" Rosalind asked.

"Yes, ma'am. I grew up around some of the best Thoroughbreds in the country." Snagging a small handful of the spiced, roasted nuts, he wandered over and took up position beside Laurel's chair. She instantly felt better.

Of course her father wasn't content to let the conversation stay on anyone else for long. "I spoke to Roger Pike yesterday. Why haven't you called him back to formally accept the job in New York?"

The mac and cheese bite turned to ash on her tongue. Laurel swallowed, washing it down with a sip of her wine. Now was the moment to speak up. To finally be honest for once. But she just... couldn't. The whole situation had turned into Mount Vesuvius when Logan did it. She wasn't looking forward to a repeat.

She and Sebastian had put off discussing a timeline until they could go over the whole idea for the center with her brother. She'd agreed because she wanted the rest of the details worked out before she even broached the topic with her parents, so she could tell them rather than sound like she was asking for permission. But that whole conversation was so big, and she hadn't felt right hitting Logan up with it the moment he got home from his honeymoon. Maybe she ought to wait until after Christmas, so as not to spoil the actual holiday. There was no reason for Athena and Logan to be subjected to her father's wrath, and it was only another two days.

"Because it's Christmas, for one. And that aside, I don't know if I'm going to accept the job."

Her father's brow drew down into a forbidding scowl that would have intimidated a witness on the stand "What do you mean you don't know if you're going to accept the job? Of course you're going to accept it. It's an excellent opportunity. It's—"

Laurel interrupted, drawing on the poise that had been

drummed into her practically from birth. "I'm at the top of my class. Carson, Danvers, Herbert, and Pike will not be my only offer. You can't expect me to jump at the first thing that comes up, no matter how amazing, without seeing what else is out there. That's hardly responsible decision making."

Her dad stared for a long time, as if he could see into her. How many defendants had simply spilled their guts under this gaze? "You have your sights set on something else?"

Laurel sensed Sebastian edging closer. She could give this piece of truth. "I do."

Lawrence broke into a wide grin. "You're going for number one."

Of course he would think that. Unwilling to drop the bomb that would destroy the tenuous peace, she sipped at her wine. "I'm keeping my options open." It wasn't an outright lie, but it still made her stomach roil to know what she was putting off.

"That's my girl. Hold out for the best."

The best for me, at least. "I've got time to make a decision. There's still my last semester to get through."

"Of course, of course. What are you taking this spring?"

It was natural to talk about heading back, what classes she'd be taking, which professors she was excited about. There was relief in not having to lie about that. Much as she didn't want to be a lawyer, she'd actually enjoyed most of law school. She liked learning, and she'd been waiting for years to take a couple of these classes. It wouldn't be a hardship to take the time and finish. Without the pressure of the job decision hanging over her head, she could simply enjoy the learning process.

Didn't that make the most sense? It was one semester and then she'd have her degree, just in case. Whether she ever used it formally or not, surely having those credentials would be beneficial when looking to woo prospective sponsors for the equine therapy center. She wouldn't feel quite so much like she'd wasted all those years, all that effort, and she'd theoretically catch less flack from her parents than if she walked away this close to the end. There was a part of her—a big part—that eased at that idea. If she finished, she wouldn't be making a prospectively irrevocable mistake, and she'd know beyond a shadow of a doubt that she was making the right decision about the rest of her life.

~

THE CALM SEBASTIAN habitually wore like a cloak evaporated, and his hands curled to fists before he forced them to relax.

She was going back to school. Going back on everything she'd said. When push came to shove, when it was time for her to actually stand up for herself and confront her father, she couldn't escape conditioning. All her talk about the therapy program, about expansion, research, and funding, was nothing more than Laurel spinning dreams so she wouldn't have to think about going back to school. But clearly, even if she didn't want the law, she wanted her parents' approval more than she wanted their dream. She was leaving, exactly as he'd known she would.

He couldn't stay here, couldn't just act like everything was fine and she hadn't just ripped his heart out. Fixing what he hoped was a neutral expression on his face, he interrupted. "I'm sorry, I need to slip out and take care of some things with the horses. Mr. and Mrs. Maxwell, it was nice to see you again. Athena, thanks for the snacks."

Did they hear the edge to his voice?

Laurel certainly did. He could feel her eyes on him, her worry a palpable thing, but he didn't look at her. Couldn't and maintain his tenuous control. He was out of the house and headed for the barn before his temper could boil over.

He'd known. From day one, he'd *known* this would happen. He'd known getting involved with her was a bad idea, but he'd let himself believe, let himself hope, that this time—with her—it would be different. That this time, he would be enough. But, of course, he wasn't. He never had been. The whole thing had been a fantasy for her, not something real. Not the way it was for him. He'd been a damned fool for investing in it, in her. She'd promised she'd stay, and at the first test, she immediately flipped her position. How could he take anything she said at face value?

Laurel cornered him in the barn. "What's wrong?"

He didn't even try to dial back the temper, didn't have it in him to try to cobble together some more control. "What's wrong? What's *wrong?* Are you kidding me right now?"

"I'm really not. What are you so angry about?" How could she stand there looking so fucking *calm?*

"You. This whole time you've been paying lip service to the idea of making a change, making a new choice, choosing something else. Choosing me. And the moment you have to confront the reality of doing the hard thing—the thing you claimed to want, you back down."

Her brows drew together. "I'm not backing down."

"Bullshit. What the hell do you call that back there?"

"Strategy. I'm not going to start a war and ruin Christmas over this. That's not fair to Athena and Logan."

"Is that really what this is? Because it seems like you're just going to put it off and put it off, quelling in the face of your father every time and chickening out."

"I'm not chickening out. We agreed to wait until we'd had the opportunity to talk things through with Logan. That was *your* stipulation. And I'm fine with that because I'm not about to announce to my parents that I'm changing my whole life without being able to present an airtight plan for what I'm doing instead. That would be tantamount to me going into court with zero preparation and expecting to win the case."

But this wasn't a case. This was his life. The lives of his animals. Now that he was free of the dream she'd woven, he realized exactly how huge a leap he was willing to take—and on what certainty? Absolutely none. He could lose all of it on her whim.

"You're going back to school."

Her eyes lightened with comprehension. "Is that what this is about?"

"You said you were going to walk away. That you wanted to stay."

"I do want to stay. But I never said I wasn't going to finish school. I only have one semester to go and then I have my degree."

"For the career you don't want."

"I'm not going to just throw away my education. As Ivy said, there are a lot of things you can do with a law degree besides courtrooms and contracts. It's foolish to come this far, to have worked this hard, and not finish what I started. Finishing school is not taking the job."

"Sure, you say that now. And what happens in five months when you graduate and you've got that shitpile of job offers from big firms and your dad is pushing you to take them? What then?"

She angled her head, eyes faintly narrowed, as if she was having to explain this all to a simpleton. "Then I walk away. By then I'll have the details figured out for what, exactly, I'm doing."

As long as he'd believed she was staying, as long as he'd been invested in the dream of them running the program together, he'd been fine. But the cold reality was that she could change her mind at any time, leaving him with something he had neither the desire nor the ability to handle.

Hell no.

She took a step toward him. "Baby, we'll figure out the details. It'll be okay."

"I can't do this." The words came out in a whisper. A truth he didn't want to voice.

"I didn't hear you. What?"

Sebastian shook his head. "I can't do this again. I can't change my whole life on the off-chance that you'll—"

"That I'll what?"

That you'll love me. That I'll be enough for you. "That you'll stay.

That you won't take off because you got a better offer, or because your dad threatened to disown you, or because you decide that this isn't what you want either."

She stared at him, a mix of emotions he couldn't read flickering over her face. "You don't trust me. That's what this is. You don't trust that I'll keep my word."

How could he? They barely knew each other. Certainly they had physical intimacy, even friendship and affection. But they didn't have history. There was no track record that she'd do anything but what she'd always done. He'd poured so much of himself, his belief, into this fantasy she'd spun for him, and it was all built on a foundation made of shifting sands.

"Do you seriously believe that I'd put all this effort into something I have no intention of following through on?" she demanded.

"I don't think you're lying." He didn't doubt that her heart was in the right place. "I think you fully intended to do this when you came up with the idea."

"I fully intend to do it now."

"I think you think you do."

Sebastian knew the moment she lapsed into lawyer mode. Her shoulders straightened and a battle light came into her eyes. "But I'm not smart enough to know my own mind?"

"It's got nothing to do with intelligence. But you spent literally years denying your instincts. How do you know you really want the life you've painted with me? Maybe it's just the more appealing of the two options." That was hardly a contest. But it didn't mean it was what she wanted for the rest of her life.

"I'm not sure which one of us you just insulted more."

"Just calling it like I see it."

"Then you're fucking blind. Do you have any idea how much trust it's taken me to get this far? You've been right here with me for the past two weeks. You know exactly how terrifying all of this is for me. I am taking this leap, giving up everything I planned, everything I've worked for, because of you. Because you were with me. You've supported me every step of the way. And that was all good and fine for you, because all the concessions were mine. But the moment you need to give a little, you're not willing to meet me halfway. You're not even willing to try because you're so afraid."

"What the hell are you talking about?" He was a fucking Ranger. He wasn't afraid.

Hands fisted, she faced him. "You're so terrified of being abandoned again, you won't even take the chance on me, on us. You're standing there inventing a problem where there was none to create a self-fulfilling prophecy, so you can tell yourself you were right. That everybody leaves, including me."

Temper sparked. That wasn't what he was doing. And he wasn't about to apologize for wanting to protect himself before getting in any further over his head. Not trusting himself to speak, he kept his mouth shut.

At his silence, she simply nodded, as if he'd confirmed something. "That's what I thought."

Without another word, she turned on her heel and strode back to the house. He didn't try to stop her.

As soon as she disappeared inside, he stalked to his truck. He didn't even know where he was going other than away. Away from the farm, away from the damned if he did and damned if he didn't decision awaiting him there. He didn't realize he was going to Harrison and Ivy's until he stood on the porch, still vibrating with fury.

Harrison opened the door, took one look at his face and called out, "Ivy! Get the good whiskey!"

CHAPTER 11

*A*s she came back into the living room, her all too intuitive brother searched her face. "Everything okay, Pip?"

"I'm fine." She wasn't anywhere close to fine. But she was determined to get through the next three days if it killed her.

Pain spread out from her sternum, and she couldn't quite stop herself from rubbing at the ache. What a perfect fucking time for an anxiety attack.

Frowning, Logan touched her shoulder. "Do you need a few minutes? I can—"

"Drop it," she snapped, her harsh tone at odds with his murmured concern. She couldn't take kindness and concern right now. She'd crumble.

Her stubborn, bull-headed lover was torpedoing their relationship before they could do more than get started. The moment they were confronted with the reality of normal life, their little bubble of happiness had shattered. She didn't know if this was just a fight or if he was really so entrenched in his abandonment issues that he couldn't even give them a real chance. The idea that she'd already lost him cut her to the quick. Grief and anxiety were a toxic mix, flooding her system, tightening the vise around her ribs. Maybe she should take a few minutes.

"You know, Laurel, if you're going to hold out for a higher ranked firm, you'll really have to find a way to step things up this semester. Have you considered—"

Her father's words beat against the fragile glass barrier holding back the tide of her frustration, until she cracked under the pressure. "Stop it!"

Her shout startled him enough that he cut off mid-sentence.

"Just stop it. Can't we go for even an hour without you pushing me to do what you want, *be* what you want? Do you even care what I want? Or is this all just some weird wish fulfillment for you?"

"What are you talking about?"

"I'm talking about my future. *My* future. *Mine.* My *life.* I haven't said yes to Carson, Danvers, Herbert, and Pike because I don't want the job. I don't want any job in New York because I don't want to practice that kind of law. I'm not even sure I want to be an attorney at all."

"How can you say that?"

"Because I can't *do* this anymore, Dad."

He drew himself up to his full height, deliberately looming in a way that should have cowed her. "You can and you will. You're just getting cold feet. You'll be a brilliant attorney."

"Yeah, I could be. And I'd hate it. Because that's not my dream. That's *your* dream, Dad. And it's my own damned fault for caring so much about your attention and approval, that I let you push me into it. But I can't live like this. Not anymore. I'm done."

"After everything I've done for you, how can you waste this opportunity?"

"How can you expect me to waste my life doing something I'd hate?"

His brows drew down like a thundercloud, and for a fleeting

moment, Laurel wondered whether he'd call out "Objection!" The idea had a hysterical laugh bubbling in the back of her throat.

"And what, exactly, are you planning to do instead? You'll just throw away your education? How will you support yourself?"

"I don't know!" she shouted. "But my trust will give me time to figure it out."

"Of all the irresponsible—"

Logan stepped between them, hands raised in peace. "Let's everybody calm down."

Lawrence rounded on him. "Calm down? Calm down? This is your influence. You did this."

Laurel wasn't about to let her brother take the heat. "Logan did nothing of the kind."

"You weren't like this until you came up here to stay." His eyes narrowed with suspicion. "It's that horse trainer. He's filled your head with foolishness. I saw the way you looked at him. Don't go throwing away your future for some...some...fling." His cheeks went ruddy with anger and embarrassment.

Stunned at his observation, it took Laurel a moment to muster a reply, and by then she knew her hesitation had given her away. "Sebastian's done nothing but let me be myself. Which is more than I can say for you."

"I have never done anything but be supportive of you."

"Yeah. You've bent over backward for me...as long as it was for something *you* wanted. But before I announced an intention to pursue the law, you couldn't be bothered to pay any attention to me. All your focus was on Logan and pushing him down the path you expected him to take."

"That's not true."

Laurel ignored his protest and kept on rolling. She was in it now. She might as well get it all out. "And from the moment he defied you, all you have done is make snide, cutting remarks about his choice, denigrating him at every turn. Do you even care what a success he's made of this place?"

"As a laborer," Lawrence spat.

"Actually, no, not just as a laborer. What Logan's accomplished here also took a truckload of brains, vision, and guts. But what the hell is wrong with physical labor? It's good, honest work. Why should you have such contempt about it?"

"Because I raised you both better than that," he bellowed. "I did not work myself to the bone to have my children throw the gift of good educations and a better position in life away."

Laurel stared at him. "Grandpa would be so disappointed in you right now."

"Then at least we'd finally have something in common."

"Lawrence!" Rosalind finally interjected, one hand clutching the pearls at her throat as she laid the other on his arm.

But no intervention was going to save things now. Eyes burning, chest constricting, Laurel just stared her father down. "Fine. At least we understand each other." Whirling away, she headed for the door.

"Where the hell do you think you're going, young lady? Don't you walk away from me."

"I'm not walking. I'm riding." She resisted the urge to slam the door in an adolescent pique—barely.

It took three tries to get her arms shoved into the coat she'd grabbed on the way out. Her hands were shaking too badly. She'd done it. She'd told her father off. Everything was out, in possibly the worst possible fashion. She'd been accusatory and disrespectful in the extreme. No matter that what she'd said was true. If he spoke to her again after all this, she'd be amazed.

Sebastian's truck was gone.

Fine. She didn't feel like seeing him right now, either. One crisis at a time.

The sky was a solid sheet of gray. Not the most pleasant weather for riding, but she wasn't in this for a happy jaunt. She needed to cool off, to gain some space and some distance so she could breathe again and figure out what the hell to do next. If they got rained on, they got rained on. They wouldn't melt.

Inside the barn, she retrieved a saddle and bridle from the tack room and went to tack up Ginger. The mare blew out a breath, bumping Laurel against the shoulder and demanding chin scratches.

"I will give you the mother of all rubdowns when we get back, pretty girl. But right now, we need to move."

She half expected Logan to come out after her, but he was probably dealing with the fallout she'd left behind. She'd apologize to him and Athena both when she returned. Swinging into the saddle, she nudged Ginger into a canter.

"AT THE FIRST sign of confrontation, she backed right down. The opportunity was *right there,* and instead of speaking up, she just started talking about next semester and going back to school, as if we hadn't made all these plans. Like she hadn't just told me she was going to change her whole life because she wanted to stay." Like she hadn't made love to him after in that very same room. "Suddenly staying with me is throwing away her education."

Frowning, Ivy crossed her legs and sank back onto the sofa. "I have a really hard time imagining Laurel saying that."

"Well, she did. She said she wasn't going to throw away her education. That it was stupid to come this far, work this hard, and not finish what she started."

Ivy pressed her lips together. "Well, sweetie, she's not wrong."

Sebastian scowled, and she held up a hand in peace.

"It does make sense for her to finish up since she only has one semester left. And probably having that law degree would impress prospective investors or donors. But I'm not hearing anything in there that staying with you would be wasting her life. It just sounds like she needs to finish this one thing. Did she ever actually *say* she wasn't going back to school?"

He opened his mouth to say yes, then stopped. They hadn't actually talked about specifics yet. It had all been put off until they could speak to Logan about all of it. Which was exactly what she'd said when he'd confronted her in the barn.

"It doesn't change anything. There's not a damned thing stopping her from walking away and dumping this whole equine therapy program in my lap."

He'd promised himself years ago he wouldn't do this again. Wouldn't do something he wasn't a hundred percent on board with just in the name of getting someone to invest in him. He knew first-hand that people couldn't be counted on. That people would always, always leave. And here he was, all ready to throw himself into this plan he'd been uncomfortable with from the start in the name of keeping Laurel in his life.

Harrison leaned forward, bracing his forearms on his knees. "Sebastian, man, she's not Kevin."

"What does he have to do with anything?"

"Look, I've known you for a lot of years. You have always been the go-to guy when anybody needs anything. You're really good at being what other people need. But in all that time, I don't think I've ever seen you ask anybody for more than helping you carry something from one place to another. Hell, you didn't even do that if you didn't have to. You don't ask people for help. Not for anything. And given your background, that makes sense. The last time you did that, your stepfather just threw up his hands and said he was out. The guy you should have been able to count on let you down, and you've spent the past decade plus expecting everybody else to do the same.

"Now here comes Laurel. She snuck right through all those defenses of yours to hand you exactly what you need. You didn't have to ask. Didn't have to say a thing. She just saw and gave, and that's so different from what you expect, you can't quite believe it.

And I get it. It's hard to get over that past experience. But at some point, you've gotta risk trusting somebody again."

Ivy leaned forward. "Laurel isn't with you because she needs something from you. She's with you because she wants to be. And she wouldn't have brought up this whole idea if she didn't intend to stick with it, to stick with *you*, to make it a success. Because that's not who she is. On some level you know that, or you wouldn't be in love with her in the first place."

Sebastian closed his eyes. He couldn't deny it. He was in love with Laurel. And it scared him shitless because she was the first person he'd let close enough to hurt him in years.

He thought about that last accusation she'd hurled at him.

You're so terrified of being abandoned again, you won't even take the chance on me, on us. You're standing there inventing a problem where there was none to create a self-fulfilling prophecy, so you can tell yourself you were right. That everybody leaves, including me.

Was that really what he was doing?

He played their entire fight back through his head, actually hearing what she'd said instead of what he'd believed. She'd never lied. She hadn't gone back on her word. They simply hadn't been on the same page. And in his haste, his fear, at the first sign of difficulty, he'd broken faith with her. She'd trusted him to be there for her while she faced her parents, and *he'd* been the one to bail. He hadn't heard her out, hadn't stuck around long enough to calm down and listen. He'd just walked away.

What kind of man did that make him?

On a sigh, Sebastian scrubbed both hands over his face. "Shit. I screwed up."

Harrison offered a wry smile. "Well, I mean, in your defense, you've never had these feelings before. This whole being in love thing can be tough."

"He's not wrong. You wouldn't be the first one to make an assumption and take off without leaving a forwarding address."

"So to speak," Harrison added.

They shared one of those private smiles that made Sebastian's gut ache.

"The point is," Ivy continued, "misunderstandings happen, but they can be forgiven. Because love."

"You just gotta man up, track her down, and tell her you're sorry." Harrison slipped an arm around Ivy's waist.

She tipped her head to his shoulder. "Don't let her wait, Sebastian. Go find your girl."

INSTINCT HAD her following the path she'd taken with Sebastian that first day. She wanted that top-of-the-world view, to make her and her problems feel small. Right now it felt as if they'd crush her. By the time she and Ginger hit the base of the mountain trail, some of the tension in her chest had eased and her mind began to process more than adrenaline and temper.

Had she lost everything? At the very least, she'd done irreparable damage to her relationship with her father. Probably with her mother, too, as Rosalind always sided with her husband. And Sebastian... Her father hadn't been entirely wrong. He'd been part of the impetus for all of this. Where did they stand?

How could he possibly be so quick to assume she'd go back on her word? She could understand how he'd thought that in the moment, but he hadn't even been willing to hear her out. His default had been to retreat instead of working through it. What did that say about their ability to weather the storm? If they couldn't come back from this, then he wasn't the man she believed him to be. The idea of that—that she'd upended her entire world for an illusion—made her ache in whole new ways. Was a life being true to herself really worth it without him in it?

At the fork in the trail, Ginger pulled left and Laurel let the mare have her head. For long minutes, she lost herself in the bunch and flex of the horse beneath her as she picked her way up the rocky slope. As the trees began to thin, Laurel looked out, expecting to see the first hints of the view, but nothing looked familiar. She must have taken a wrong turn somewhere.

"It's fine. We just need to make a U-turn and head back down."

Ginger's ears swiveled back at the sound of her voice.

The trail was too narrow to reverse. "Okay, we'll just keep going. As soon as we get to a spot big enough to turn around, we will."

The mare quivered beneath her. She needed to get her own nerves under control so as not to make things worse. "Easy. Easy girl. We're gonna get out of this and then go on back. I'll give you a nice, long massage with that nubby brush you like so much."

Thunder boomed so close Laurel felt the vibration in the air. Ginger screamed and lurched, scrambling up the rocky path at breakneck speed. Laurel lost a stirrup, but maintained her seat, gripping tight with her knees as she tried to regain control. But Ginger was too far gone to heed any commands. Incoherent prayers tumbled through Laurel's head as she held on for dear life.

Another clap of thunder shook the mountain, and Ginger reared. With a scream, Laurel slipped from the saddle, falling, falling. She landed with a bone-jarring crunch at the edge of the rocky trail. The ground collapsed beneath her, her lower half sliding over the side.

She scrabbled for purchase, fingers digging, feet flailing. She snagged a spindly sapling growing out of the rock and jerked to a halt, jarring her shoulder. On a sob, she sucked in a breath of relief. Shoving back the panic, she reached up to grab the tree with both hands, pedaling her feet to search for some kind of footing.

Oh God. Oh God. Oh God.

But her feet found nothing, and as her body continued to thrash, the roots pulled free, and she dropped like a stone off the side of the mountain.

CHAPTER 12

*H*is girl. As he drove back to the farm, he sure as hell hoped that was still accurate. Maybe with an apology, this would be their first fight and not their last.

The sky stretched out in an endless gray sheet. He didn't like the look of the clouds boiling above the hills. That storm would be cresting the mountain soon. It would hit the valley and the farm not long after that. He needed to get the horses fed and rounded up, and prepare to sleep light tonight in case Ginger lost her shit. With that in mind, he pulled up in front of the barn.

Almost as soon as he stopped, people were spilling out of the house. The tension slammed into him, setting him on alert even before Lawrence Maxwell stormed over.

"You! This is all your fault."

So Laurel had finally told him. Good for her.

Pocketing his keys, Sebastian kept his expression placid. "Excuse me?"

Logan tried to step between them. "Dad, calm down."

Lawrence ignored him, instead stepping into Sebastian's space and jabbing him in the shoulder with one finger. "She's never been reckless a day in her life and two weeks with you and suddenly she's throwing away everything she's worked for. And for what?"

It took all Sebastian's self-restraint not to dislocate that finger and drop the man to his knees, so there wasn't any left to hold back his temper. Straightening to his full height, he loomed over the older man. "For a chance to fucking breathe," he growled. "Do you have any idea what she's been going through these past few years? She's bent over backward, pushed herself until she's had panic attacks, all in the name of trying to earn your approval—which you ought to be giving her either way because she's goddamned amazing, no matter what she chooses to do."

"She's throwing her life away, and I won't have it."

"It's not your decision to make. She's a grown woman, who's more than capable of making her own decisions—or would be if you'd stop manipulating your kids by only giving them attention when they're doing what you want. A parent is supposed to fucking be there, be supportive, and actually listen and give a shit what their kid wants, not try to turn them into a carbon copy or shove their own agenda down their kid's throat."

An angry flush crept up the other man's face. "How dare you presume—"

"For God's sake, Dad!" Logan snapped. "Even now, you're more interested in winning this argument and making your point than in what's important. Sebastian, Laurel is missing."

"What?"

"She hasn't come back."

"What are you talking about?"

"Laurel. She was upset, and she went out for a ride more than an hour ago. She hasn't come back."

Thunder rolled across the valley.

Oh no. Oh fuck. He knew. Even before he heard the sound of pounding hooves, he knew.

Ginger came flying through the north pasture, stirrups bouncing, saddle empty.

As the bottom fell out of his world, Sebastian moved to intercept her, waving his arms. She nearly mowed him down, but reared at the last moment. Darting in, he snagged the trailing reins, moving with her when she shied.

"Whoa. Whoa. Easy. Settle."

He slowly reeled her in until he could get his hands on her quivering neck. Her eyes wheeled in terror and her breath sawed in and out like a bellows. Despite the panic blooming in his own chest, he kept his tone soft and even, soothing her until she stood still long enough for him to check her legs and feet. There were several nicks along her fetlocks and stones in her hooves. If she didn't come up lame tomorrow, it would be a miracle.

"Logan, saddle Brego."

He was already moving toward the barn. "Who else?"

"No one else."

"What? But we have to find her. She could be hurt or…"

"Don't finish that sentence." Slowly, Sebastian led Ginger toward the barn. "I'm going after her. But there's a storm coming, and it'll be dark in half an hour. I'm not having any more of the horses or inexperienced riders injured by going out in it."

"You're not having it? What gives you the right to make that call? That's my daughter out there!" Lawrence demanded. But there was fear underneath the anger now.

Sebastian resisted the urge to point out that if he'd been less of a dick, Laurel wouldn't be out there at all. The same could easily be said of him, too. "Because I'm an Army Ranger. I'm trained for search and rescue. None of the rest of you are."

Turning his back on Laurel's father, he narrowed his focus on the task in front of him, clearing the stones and stripping off the saddle and bridle from the terrified mare. "Okay, girl. We're done. You're safe." He turned her loose, watching her run straight to the three-walled shelter.

"Athena, call Xander. Have him put search and rescue on stand-by." Not waiting to see if she moved, he bolted for his cabin.

His mind spun with scenarios for how Ginger ended up back here without her rider and almost none of them were good. He prayed Laurel had just dismounted to check the mare's feet and lost hold of the reins when she spooked. It was the only variation he could envision that didn't involve her getting thrown and sustaining a multitude of injuries. Shrugging into rain gear, he grabbed the pack he kept stocked and ready for search and rescue missions. He'd only been called out a handful of times since he'd joined the local SAR team, and that had been for simple, successful searches. This was a whole other level of fear because this was personal.

Be okay, damn it. Wherever you are, just hang on. I'm coming.

In less than five minutes, he was back, shifting supplies and bedroll from the pack into his saddle bags.

"Are you packing to camp?" Lawrence asked incredulously.

"If I have to. I don't know what I'm going to find, and if I'm on the mountain after dark, it won't be safe to bring my horse back down."

Athena hurried up from the house. "Xander is mobilizing the team."

"Let's pray we don't need them." But the temperature was dropping and the rain would be here any minute. Sebastian swung into the saddle. "Take the 4x4 and the truck and check everything you can drive to. I'll be checking the places you can't drive. My radio is on, though there may be interference from the storm. Let's keep each other posted, as best as we can. If I find her after dark and can't get through, I've got a flare gun."

"What else can we do?" White-faced, Laurel's mother wrapped both arms around her middle.

Sebastian didn't have any softness or false hope. "Pray."

Digging his heels into Brego's flanks, he galloped off to find the woman he loved.

∼

EVERYTHING HURT.

Why the hell did she feel like she'd gone three rounds with Mike Tyson? And why was it so damned cold?

Opening her eyes, Laurel frowned, her brain not immediately processing the field of gray clouding her vision. Blinking slowly, she tried to move. Pain lanced through her shoulder, and her skull pounded like a timpani drum.

What the hell?

Thunder boomed all too close, jolting her fully back to consciousness. Ginger. The storm. She'd been thrown.

Oh my God.

Urgency beat in her blood as she scrambled to her knees. One hand slipped. On instinct, she threw herself in the opposite direction to keep from face planting, and saw the drop. Terror stole her ability to scream, but she scrambled back, pressing as tightly to the rock face as possible. By some miracle, she'd landed on a narrow ledge of rock instead of plummeting all the way to the bottom. Her perch wasn't more than about three feet deep. If she'd rolled the other way or slipped just a few feet further to the left or right, she'd have missed it entirely.

Lungs seizing, she fought back the panic. Panic wouldn't get her out of this situation.

In through the nose, out through the mouth.

Thunder rolled again. She couldn't stay here. The storm would hit any minute now.

Still moderating her breathing, Laurel assessed her injuries. Her shoulder seemed to be the worst of it. Careful rolling of the joint proved it was wrenched, not dislocated. She definitely had a multitude of bruises and abrasions, and obviously she'd struck her head, but nothing seemed to be broken. She could climb.

A single look back up the way she'd come disabused her of that notion. The trail was at least fifteen or twenty feet up. The rock face itself was almost vertical, with no easy handholds. Maybe, if she had some kind of a rope, but she had nothing. There was no sign of Ginger, and Laurel could only hope the mare had made it safely off the mountain and that she'd run home to alert someone.

"Help!" She shouted it, and her voice echoed off the walls of the stone. "Help me!"

The sky answered with a bullwhip crack of thunder and split open, pelting her with freezing rain. She was soaked in less than a minute, chattering in under two. How long did it take to die of exposure? Did anyone even realize she was gone?

Maybe she could climb or slide down to safer ground below. She scooted forward just far enough to see over the lip. The only way down was a long drop. Because she had to do something, she kept shouting between rumbles of thunder. But no one came. Who could hear her way up here? As darkness fell, the futility of her situation had tears coursing down her cheeks, mixing with the freezing rain.

If she'd handled everything better, she wouldn't be in this mess. If she'd come clean to her father in a calm, rational presentation, she wouldn't have lost her temper—probably. She definitely wouldn't have fought with Sebastian. And she wouldn't have ridden out alone. Regret weighed on her as much as her sodden clothes.

There'd be no chance to fix any of it. Even if people were out looking for her, who could search in all this? They wouldn't even know where to look. At best, she'd be hypothermic well before morning. At worst...she wasn't quite ready to think about the worst. Because the worst meant never seeing Sebastian again. Never telling him she loved him.

She wasn't ready to give up yet.

Please, God. Please, show me the way. Don't let this be the end.

But as the cold seeped into her very marrow, no answer appeared. The hands she'd shoved under her armpits had gone past cold, past pain, and into numb. So had her feet. Even if she'd wanted to risk climbing in the dark, she'd never be able to hold on to anything now. The rain continued to drum, stinging her cheeks. Then she stopped feeling even that as her body slid into what she knew was dangerously cold territory. Was she even shivering anymore? Laurel couldn't tell. It got hard to keep her eyes open, hard to keep track of the endless, wet night.

When her body slid, tipping over to one side, she couldn't even catch herself. There was no muscle control. No more will. Not even more sense of cold. She was past that. In some dark recess of her mind, a tiny voice was screaming for her to wake up, sit up, do something to get the blood flowing, to generate warmth. But she was beyond able to listen.

Maybe freezing wouldn't be the worst way to go.

Laurel.

Her brain was shouting at her again, louder this time. Deeper, too. When had her inner voice started to sound like Sebastian? She'd like to dream of him as she went. She'd read somewhere that freezing wasn't such a bad way to die. That you just went to sleep and didn't wake up again.

"Laurel!" The voice was louder this time. That definitely sounded like Sebastian. And he sounded...close? But that was impossible. Wasn't it?

With great effort, she pried her eyes open in time to see the bright arc of a shooting star. Was it lighting her way to heaven?

She listened, straining to hear her name again, but there was nothing. Closing her eyes again, she tried to find her way into the dream. At least there she could say what was in her heart.

"Laurel! Jesus God." And then he was there, her beautiful, badass angel, wrapping her in his arms. Laurel curled into him, wanting to chase this fantasy. The fantasy was warm.

"Baby. Come on. Wake up. You need to look at me. Christ, please wake up." Dream Sebastian was freaking out. That didn't seem right. Neither did the stroke of pain along her cheek.

Forcing her eyes open one last time, she saw him. It was dark, and the outline was vague, but she'd know him anywhere. He stroked her face again.

"Ow," she groaned.

He made a noise like a wounded animal, and suddenly she was shifted as he pulled her tighter against him. Because he was *here*. Holy hell, he was really here. He'd come after her. The heart that had slowed with the cold began to thud painfully in her chest.

Sebastian.

She tried to say his name but her lips wouldn't form the word. The only sound that escaped was a whimper.

"It's gonna be okay, baby. I've gotcha. I promise"

Beyond exhausted, her eyes fell shut again, and she sank deeper into the black.

The next time it receded, she felt the uneven rhythm of a horse. Mustering the last of her energy, she cracked her eyes open again.

She was *on* a horse. Tied to the saddle. Up ahead, a dark figure had hold of the reins, leading them up a rocky path. Sebastian. She recognized his gait. Her ears hummed with the silence, but for the clop of hooves. It was no longer raining. White swirled in the air around them. Snow?

Were they really getting a white Christmas?

Something about that struck her as funny, and she began to laugh. The sound came out more like a weak, coughing groan, but it was enough to get Sebastian's attention.

"Laurel? Are you awake?"

He was beside her in a moment, one hand on her leg. She saw it, but she couldn't feel the pressure. What did that mean?

Weaving in the saddle, she had a hard time focusing. "Sebastian? Am I alive?"

He made a choked sort noise in his throat and reached up to touch her face. "Yeah. And I'm gonna make sure you stay that way."

She felt him. The touch of his gloved fingers against her skin, a bloom of pain. Which meant he was here. Not in a dream or a hallucination, but flesh and blood. He'd saved her.

"Okay."

"Stay awake. I need you to stay with me, baby."

"Can't."

"Laurel!" She could hear the alarm and command in his voice and knew she was scaring him, but she was too tired to do more than trust that he'd carry out his promise. So she let herself slide into complete oblivion.

CHAPTER 13

*A*ll the way up the mountain, Sebastian had cursed the rain. Now he cursed the snow and the continually plummeting temperatures. They couldn't get back down in this, and Laurel wouldn't survive if he didn't get her body temperature back up. He had one shot, and he prayed with every step that it would be enough.

He almost missed the cabin in the dark. Mother Nature had made greater strides in reclaiming the old bootlegger's cabin since the spring. A sapling of some kind grew right up through the porch boards, and a whole host of overgrowth had tangled to make a natural screen. But it was still standing. Quickly tying Brego's reins to a rail, he strode up onto the porch. Many of its boards were rotted. The only door to the place was closed. The knob turned with effort, and it swung open a couple of inches before stopping. Putting his shoulder to it, he managed to make a gap wide enough to get through.

Sweeping his light, he made a quick assessment of the place. The roof was still intact. Puddles on the floor in places made it clear there were leaks, but there were no gaping holes. The wide-planked floors were a bit warped, but seemed stable. The few windows in the place had cracks, and there were a couple of missing panes. A table and two chairs occupied the front corner, by an old-fashioned wood stove. There was no other furniture, the place having been cleared out long ago, but it would get them out of the wind and snow. But what the hell to do with Brego? There was no guarantee the floorboards would stand up to his weight, and the last thing they needed was damage to his legs in the middle of all this shit.

Hurrying back outside, Sebastian circled the perimeter. And in the back struck gold. A lean-to had been constructed between the cabin and the wall of the mountain. Little more than a tin roof stretched between the two, but brush and trees made a natural screen on either side that blocked most of the wind. Getting the gelding in here would be a bit of a squeeze, but the nook it made would get him out of the worst of the weather for the night.

Laurel groaned as he untied her from the saddle and slid her down. She roused enough to curl into him as he lifted her up and carried her into the cabin. He stretched her gently on the floor.

"Don't leave me," she rasped.

His heart twisted. As if he wouldn't ride through hell all over again just to find her. "Not going anywhere. Just gotta get my pack."

He brought it inside, setting his flashlight to lantern mode and digging out a reflective blanket and self-heating handwarmers. Ripping open both packs, he shook them until they activated and unzipped her coat. She whimpered again as he peeled off her wet clothes. Her skin was icy to the touch and her lips had a bluish cast, but the worst of the injuries appeared to be scrapes and bruises, which was a fucking miracle. The danger now was complications from exposure.

"I'm sorry. I'm sorry." For so many things. But there would be time for recriminations later.

Gentle as he could, he wrapped her in the reflective blanket, tucking the warmers beneath her armpits. She needed more, but that was going to take time. His gaze moved to the wood stove. Did he dare try to start a fire? Who knew when it had last been used. The chimney could be full of birds' nests or who knew what detritus. But they needed a heat source. Finding no evidence of vermin inside it, and hearing the wind whistling through the vent above, he decided to risk it.

With quick, brutal efficiency, he shattered the chair. Breaking the remaining bits down small enough to fit into the stove, he stuffed them in and added some tinder from his pack, grateful beyond measure when it caught. As soon as he was certain it would keep burning, he returned to Laurel. Behind her closed lids, her eyes fluttered as he checked her pulse. Slow, but strong. Satisfied she'd be stable for the next few minutes, he hurried outside, trying to radio back to the farm again. Something was interfering with the signal, and he could only hope they'd seen his flare. For now, he had to deal with his horse.

Brego balked a bit as Sebastian tugged him toward the thick cluster of trees.

"Come on, big man. I know you want out of this miserable weather as much as I do. You trusted me enough to bring me up here. Trust me a little further."

Snorting, the gelding bobbed his head and stepped forward, into the trees. Once out of the wind and snow, he heaved a huge sigh, as if he realized it was finally time to rest for the night. Slicing off a cedar bough with his tactical knife, Sebastian used it to quickly brush off the snow. His mount deserved more than just this, but it would have to wait until he'd seen to Laurel.

"I'll be back to bring you some water as soon as I can." Before he went back inside, Sebastian pressed his face against Brego's neck. "Thank you. Thank you for carrying me up here, for risking your life to save hers." He gave himself a minute. Sixty little seconds to let the fear he'd been holding back for hours flood his system. That he wouldn't find her. That she'd be broken or dead.

All the horrific scenarios that had played through his head on that frantic ride.

This was his fault. He'd known that as soon as he'd seen Ginger. If he hadn't pushed Laurel, hadn't been so fucking insecure, she would have waited to break the news. It might still have turned into a shitshow, but she wouldn't have been alone. He'd have been there with her. For her. She'd have turned to him in her upset instead of riding out under poor conditions on the one horse in his stable she couldn't have known would flip out.

Knowing his time was up, he shut all of it away, compartmentalizing it to take out later, when all of this was over. He'd found her. She was safe. She was going to be okay. There were countless other things to deal with, but for now, that was all that mattered.

LAUREL WOKE to warmth and pain. Confused, she struggled through layers of sleep. Sebastian's scent surrounded her, soothing the disquiet that lingered from dreams she couldn't quite remember. One big hand cradled her head, and she could feel the faint warmth of his breath stirring the hair at her temple. Everything hurt, but tangled up with him, still more than half asleep, she couldn't find the willpower to do more than burrow closer, skin to skin.

"Laurel?"

On a groan, she tucked tighter against him. "You need a new mattress."

"You're awake. Thank God." His voice was ragged, fraught with an exhaustion and relief that didn't make any sense to her.

Dragging herself the rest of the way awake, she opened her eyes.

They weren't at his house. They weren't even in a bed. And he didn't need a new mattress. He *was* the mattress. She was stretched out atop him, wrapped tight in some kind of blanket. A sleeping bag? That would explain the restriction of movement. They lay on a hardwood floor in a room that looked like the set for an old western movie. Everything was dark but for the glow cast by an old wood stove in the corner. A bunch of clothes appeared to be laid out beside it.

"Where are we?"

"Bootlegger's cabin. It was the closest shelter when I found you."

Everything came back to her in a rush. The fall. The storm. Nearly dying.

"I thought you were a dream." But the heart that beat steadily against hers proved otherwise.

His arms tightened around her, and his voice shook. "I thought I was too late."

Given that she'd been lapsing in and out of consciousness, he probably hadn't been far from it. How much longer could she have lasted?

"I didn't think anyone could even be out looking for me in the storm. I thought I'd freeze before morning." Shivering with the memory, she snuggled closer to his heat, tangling her bare legs with his. "How did you even find me?"

"Ginger came back without you."

"She made it back? Oh, thank God." If the mare had been hurt or killed because of her foolishness, she'd never have been able to forgive herself.

"I've been through a lot of shit, faced down terrorists, arms dealers, and all sorts of enemy combatants. But I have never in my life been so scared as I was when I saw that empty saddle."

And he'd ridden into the face of a storm to come find her. No matter the harsh words they'd thrown at each other, he'd still come for her. Still risked his life to save hers.

Emotion clogged her throat. She loved this man. Totally. Completely. She'd held off telling him before, reasoning that it was too soon. But while she'd been trapped on that ledge, faced with the prospect of dying, all the logic, all the rules and bullshit had been stripped away. The only thing in her mind, as her body got colder and colder, was that she wouldn't get to see him again, wouldn't get to tell him how she felt. She wouldn't waste any more time.

Propping herself up just enough so she could look into his face, she took a breath. "Sebastian."

He curled his hand around her nape. "Wait. I need to say something."

The intensity of his gaze had her swallowing back the words again. "Okay."

"I'm sorry. I'm so fucking sorry for not trusting you. For getting all up in my own shit and—"

"We should have talked first. Before my parents ever got there. I should have made it clear to you that I was going to finish my last semester. I should have made it clear that I was going to avoid dropping the bomb about the job until after Christmas. You expected one thing, I did something else, and you reacted."

"So badly. I'm so sorry for that."

She worked her hand free to cup his cheek. "You reacted like someone who's been hurt before. Someone who put his trust in another person and got left behind. Maybe you should have believed in me, but I should have been more careful with you."

"Laurel." He drew her brow to his and she closed her eyes, feeling her world tip back to rights. They were going to be okay.

His fingers stroked down her nape, as if he needed the assurance of being able to touch her. "I feel like I need to explain this. It just got...so big. First there was the equine therapy center, then the idea of expanding the operation off Logan's farm—I wasn't sure I wanted any of it. Until you said you want to stay. To run it with me. It didn't seem so big when I saw you by my side. You're a force of nature, after all."

She couldn't help it. She snorted. One corner of his mouth lifted in a semblance of his rare smile, then he sobered again.

"The more time we spent together, the more that vision of you and me, doing this together—the more that became real to me. I don't think anything in my life has ever been so big, so real, so important. And then..."

She could see it now, where his mind had been as he'd listened to her casually chat with her father about courting other job offers for after law school. This earnest, honest man who didn't come from a life of social masks and double-speak. "And then my parents showed up, and I acted like none of it ever happened. I made you think I might just turn around and go right back to that life."

He offered a sheepish, wobbly smile and swallowed. "I felt like I'd built a castle in the air."

Her heart ached at the idea that she'd hurt him, even unintentionally. "Oh Sebastian, I'm sorry."

"No, I'm sorry. I know you, your bravery, your integrity. I should have trusted you. Trusted us. I just... I've never loved anyone before. Not the way I love you."

A bright burst of joy exploded in her chest. He loved her.

Turning her head, she pressed a kiss to his palm. "I was going to say it first. I love you, Sebastian." She watched the answering joy come into his eyes and couldn't hold back a smile. "I know there are a hundred more things we should probably discuss, but at the end of the day, the only thing that matters is that I love you, and I'm alive to say it because of you." Brushing her lips softly to his, she whispered, "Thank you for coming after me."

"I'd have ridden into hell itself to bring you home."

He kissed her, worshiping her mouth with a devastating gentleness that had her forgetting everything but the taste and feel of him. Needing more, she strained toward him and cracked her knee against the floor.

"Ow!"

Sebastian froze. "You okay?"

"You mean other than being sexually frustrated by this sleeping bag? Yeah."

He huffed a laugh. "Sorry. I wasn't setting out to seduce you. You were hypothermic. This was the safest way to get your body temperature up. It was a feat to squeeze you in here at all."

She squirmed a little to test the theory but had to concede he was right. "It's a tragic waste of nakedness. Stupid all-weather, subzero, down-filled condom."

The laugh turned full fledged, shaking them both. "I promise, I'll spend a few hours making it up to you as soon as we get home and settled."

"Home." She sighed the word, settling back against his chest, head tucked under his chin. "You know, Henry David Thoreau said, 'If you have built castles in the air, your work need not be lost; that is where they should be. Now put the foundations under them.' I want to go home with you, build the foundation for that vision you were talking about."

"The one where we live happily ever after?"

"Once we deal with my father."

His arms tightened around her, one hand going back to her nape. "Don't you worry about that. I have every confidence you can sell ice to an Eskimo. You can totally talk your dad around. And I'll be right by your side, because after this scare you'll be lucky if I let you out of my sight for the next fifty or sixty years."

She snuggled against him, feeling all the stress and strain melt away. "I'm good with that."

CHAPTER 14

"*L*ieutenant Donnelly, come in. Over."

Sebastian snapped fully awake, mentally braced for action. But he was no longer in a war zone. Not waiting for an extraction for his team. A warm weight draped over him, her hair spilling across his chest. Laurel. Beneath his palms, her back rose and fell in a slow, steady rhythm. Early dawn light filtered in through the windows of the cabin.

From somewhere to his right, the radio crackled again. "Damn it, Sebastian. Answer me." He recognized Harrison's frustrated voice.

Laurel groaned, nuzzling into his chest, even as he reached for the radio. His bare skin pebbled to instant gooseflesh. The fire had gone out sometime in the night.

"Good morning to you, too, Captain."

"Thank Christ. Status?"

"We're both okay. What are you doing on this channel?"

"Sheriff briefed us last night. They saw your flare but when nobody could raise you on the radio, we were ready to roll come first light in case the situation called for it. "

"Negative. I'll be able to get her down myself."

"Do either of you need medical?"

Laurel shifted propping her chin on his pec and blinking at him with sleepy hazel eyes.

"She should probably get checked out, just in case, but it's not ER worthy. We'll be on our way as soon as I can get gear packed up. Whoever mobilized can go on home."

"Roger that."

A new voice came over the line. "Can we talk to her?"

At the sound of it, Laurel lost the bonelessness of sleep.

Sebastian took his finger off the mic button. "I know you may not want to talk to your dad right now, but he probably needs to hear your voice. And if not him, your mom and Logan and Athena will."

On a sigh, Laurel nodded. "Dad?"

The silence stretched out so long, Sebastian wondered if the radio had gone out again.

"Are you okay, baby?"

Her lips pressed into a line. "I'm alive and all in one piece."

Did her father recognize she hadn't answered the question?

"Thank God." Laurel's brows drew down at the shaking in his voice. Sebastian was willing to bet Lawrence Maxwell wasn't prone to displays of emotion.

"Thank Sebastian." Her words held the whip of a closing argument. "We'll see y'all when we get down the mountain."

"Donnelly out."

Before he even set the radio aside, she was attacking the zipper and scrambling out of the sleeping bag. As the frigid air hit his skin, he wanted to swear. But other than hunching her shoulders, Laurel didn't make a peep of complaint as she hustled across to where he'd laid their clothes out by the stove last night.

"Are they dry?"

"A little crunchy, but yeah." She shimmied into hers almost before he rolled out of the bag, but he still noted the assortment of bruises painting her skin. They were a stark reminder of what she'd been through.

The images that evoked left him feeling gut-punched over everything that might have happened. So many variations where she didn't come out of this alive. Where he was too late. Where he'd failed.

"Sebastian." Laurel's arms came around him and he buried his face in her hair. "What's wrong?"

"Nothing. I just—" He held her close, careful not to squeeze too tight. "You could have died."

"But I didn't. I'm safe and whole because of you. I'm okay."

He pulled back far enough to study her face. "*Are* you okay? You seem…a little off."

She ducked her chin. "I'm just dreading facing everyone. I feel stupid for riding off like that. Like I had a tantrum and did something reckless, and messed up everyone's Christmas."

Shit. It's Christmas Day. In all the chaos, he'd forgotten.

"You didn't know Ginger has a phobia of storms. And I'm pretty sure whatever you said to your dad—however you said it— was justified. Speaking of, you should know he and I, uh, had some words before I left."

"Oh?"

"He came out verbally swinging when I got back. Apparently I'm a bad influence on you. I let him know exactly what I think about his treatment of you, so I'm probably not his favorite person at the moment."

"The saving my life part should probably mitigate that." She tipped her mouth up to his for a soft kiss. "Thank you for standing up for me."

"Always."

Her stomach gave a monstrous growl, and she laughed. "I can't wait for food!"

Sebastian dug out an energy bar and some water. "Here. Work on these. I'll go saddle Brego."

He made quick work of it, leading the gelding back around to the front of the cabin to load up the rest. Checking the stove one last time to make certain the coals were all the way out, he finished loading the saddle bags and helped Laurel mount. Once he swung into the saddle behind her, she leaned her back against his chest, resting one arm over the one he'd circled around her waist.

"Let's go home," she sighed.

Home. That was right here in his arms.

The ride down took longer than he wanted, but at two-up, he didn't want to strain Brego any worse than necessary. As they hit the farm road that circled up past the north pasture and beyond, the gelding picked up the pace.

"The siren song of breakfast," Sebastian observed.

"I could definitely still go for that myself. And a shower and clean clothes. Not necessarily in that order."

Conversation turned to fantasies about what kind of food they were dreaming about.

"Surely we can sweet-talk Athena into cooking for us. I mean, what's the point of having a sister-in-law who's an award-winning chef if I can't beg for..." Laurel trailed off as they topped the rise and the house came into view. Cars were everywhere, parked cheek-by-jowl all in front of the barn and farmhouse. At least a couple dozen people milled about in the yard.

"I thought you sent everybody home."

"So did I." Sebastian scanned the vehicles, recognizing several belonging to search and rescue team members. "Guess they needed to see for themselves that we're okay."

Someone evidently spotted them because a cheer went up from the assembly.

"You ready for this?" he asked.

"Do I have a choice?"

"Probably not." He tightened his grip around her waist. "I'll be right beside you."

"Holding you to that."

Logan, Harrison, Ty, and Porter were at the head of the pack as they rode into the yard, stopping just far enough away that Brego didn't balk at being crowded. The elder Maxwells spilled out of the house as Sebastian dismounted. Lawrence looked like hell, his steel gray hair standing on end, and lines carved deep around his eyes and mouth. The night had aged him a decade. Laurel's gaze flicked to her parents, uncertainty in her expression before she blanked it and reached for Sebastian. He lifted her down from the saddle, automatically wrapping her in the shelter of his arms as he met Lawrence Maxwell's eyes.

So many threats and warnings wanted to spill out of his mouth, but Sebastian stayed silent. He was pretty sure his expression spoke for him. After a long moment, Lawrence nodded. Message received.

Then the tide of people broke over them and Laurel was tugged out of his embrace and surrounded by her family.

Brego needed seeing to, and Sebastian wanted to check on Ginger, but he kept a close eye on Laurel. He'd promised she wouldn't face this alone.

"Oh my God, I'm so glad you're both okay!" Ari burst through the crowd to throw her arms around his waist.

Sebastian rocked back on his heels, surprised by the onslaught of affection. Not sure what else to do, he ruffled her hair. "Hey, kid. What are you doing here?"

"Are you kidding? The whole family's here. Actually we're way past the whole family at this point."

"So I see. I thought everybody was disbursing after my radio transmission."

"Well, we were, and then Athena offered to feed everybody breakfast for their trouble," Harrison explained.

"Yeah, nobody's dumb enough to turn *that* down," Porter added.

"Can I take care of Brego?" Ari asked.

"That'd be great. He's had a rough night, and he'll be wanting breakfast and a good rubdown."

Ari saluted and took the reins, leading the gelding toward the stable.

His friends stepped up, one after another, pulling him into back-slapping hugs. Then came Logan.

He clasped Sebastian's hand in both of his, his eyes full of emotion. "I don't know how to thank you."

"Not necessary."

"You saved her life. How bad was it?"

There was no sense in scaring him witless after the fact. "Save those gray hairs for when you have kids. The important thing is, she's safe, and she's home."

"Lieutenant."

They both turned as Lawrence stepped up. Sebastian looked back at Laurel, who had her arms wrapped around her mother. She seemed none the worse for wear after the encounter with her father.

"Sir."

The man hesitated, then offered a hand. "Thank you for bringing her home."

Sebastian angled his head in acknowledgment.

"And I'm sorry for being a jackass."

Sebastian didn't like Lawrence Maxwell, but chances were, they were gonna be in each other's lives for a long time in the future. It'd serve him well to learn to be civil. So he took the proffered hand and angled his head in acknowledgment. "I'm not the one who deserves an apology."

The older man nodded again. "Working on it."

Well, that was a start.

WHAT I LIKE ABOUT YOU

"You're injured. You sit," Athena ordered. "Dinner's nearly ready."

"But the doctor said it was just a mild concussion," Laurel protested.

"And a sprained shoulder," Logan added. "Sit."

She started to push up from the sofa. "Then I'll help Sebastian with the evening feeding."

"Nope." The man himself leaned over to brush a kiss to her temple. "You are officially off-duty. I'll be back in a little bit."

Laurel had the sense that the last bit was as much a warning to her father as a promise to her. True to his word, he'd stayed by her side almost all day, acting as her shield. She didn't know what he'd said to her dad, but so far Lawrence had behaved himself. Still, her stomach tightened as everybody disbursed to their pre-dinner tasks, leaving her alone with him. She braced for a cross-examination, wishing alcohol wasn't off the menu for the night.

"Why didn't you tell me you were unhappy?" Her father's voice was gentle rather than accusatory—a tone she'd never heard from him.

Cautiously hopeful that this time he might actually listen, she didn't censor herself. "Seriously? You practically excommunicated Logan when he quit grad school."

He opened his mouth, and she could see him stop himself to change his answer. "Do you want to finish law school?"

"Yes." That part had never been in question for her.

"Then it's not the same."

She was beyond done with his attitude toward her brother. If she couldn't call him out on it today, when he was less likely to snap back because of what she'd been through, when could she? "Logan doesn't deserve to be punished for having a different dream than you. He finally figured out what he wanted and he went after it. And he's made it come to fruition. What he's done here is nothing short of miraculous, and it deserves respect, even if it's not the choice you'd make."

For maybe the first time in her life, her father looked...embarrassed? He heaved a sigh. "You're right."

Laurel blinked, positive she hadn't heard him correctly. "Excuse me?

"You're right. I've behaved badly—to both of you."

It was official. Hell had frozen over. Maybe she should go buy a lottery ticket.

He leaned forward, hands loosely clasped between his knees. "When I was growing up, I had nothing in common with my father. He was a working man—a dairy farmer—and I was a scholar. I resented every hour I had to spend laboring with those cows. He did the best that he could, and he supported our family, always. We never wanted for anything we needed. But I had bigger ambitions. I swore to myself I'd do better for myself, for my family. That you wouldn't have to do that kind of work, wouldn't have to sacrifice your potential in the name of just getting by. You and your brother are so smart, so capable, and it was easy to dream big dreams about what the two of you could accomplish. It was easy to pull you into mine. It hurt when Logan didn't want to do law school. I'd always imagined a father and son firm. And it was worse that he wanted to do almost the exact thing I'd tried to save him from. All those years when you were growing up, I didn't ignore you on purpose. I didn't know what to do or say to a little girl. But then you announced your interest in pursuing the law, and it was like I got a second chance. You and I jibed on that front. You've done so incredibly well, and I'm so very proud of you."

"I know. And that was why I couldn't tell you. Every single conversation we had was about school, about work, about what I would do, should do. I don't know when the pressure started to get unbearable. I think it happened so gradually, I didn't even realize until things were really bad. And then it felt like I was in too deep to change things."

His throat worked. "I should have asked you what you wanted instead of assuming it was what I wanted."

Hearing him say that was balm to some wound she'd been carting around for years. But the fault didn't lie entirely with him. "I should have asked myself. But no one asked me. Not until Sebastian."

Her father hesitated. "You...care for him."

Care seemed like too pale a word for what she felt for Sebastian, but she'd given her dad enough shocks the last twenty-four hours. "Very much."

"He's very protective of you."

"He's a good man, Dad. One of the best ones I know."

"You're going to keep him, aren't you?"

Laurel's mouth fell open. "I don't know. I hope so. But that's not entirely up to me."

His expression was caught somewhere between discomfort and approval. "He looks at you like I look at your mother."

What was she supposed to say to that?

He didn't wait for a reply. "When you finish school in May, you'll be coming back here?"

"We haven't worked out the details yet, but probably."

"And what will you do for a living? Your brother at least had a plan."

"Actually, I have a plan, and it's something I'm hoping you can help me with." The idea for this olive branch had come to her on the long drive back from the hospital in Johnson City.

"Me? What can I do?"

"I've been doing a lot of research on non-profits and grants since I've been here. Sebastian has really taken ownership of the equine rescue, but he's out of space. We're looking to move beyond that, into a bigger program that includes equine-assisted therapy. To really turn it into something, he needs his own place, and to afford that, he needs funding. So I've been looking into various grant programs, putting together packets on the ones I think are the best fit, that he has the best shot at landing. All my analytic skills and ability to understand legalese mean I've got a leg up on most people who'd even look at these grant mechanisms, let alone actually apply for them. I want to help other people through that process."

"You want to be a professional grant-writer?"

"Yeah. That's part of it. There's always a need for someone to help navigate the needless complication. And it's a thing I can do from anywhere."

"It's not what I would have imagined, but I can see how you'd be good at it. What does that have to do with me?"

"Well, I'm a Maxwell, so of course I can't stop with just that."

His lips curved. "Got a little of me in you, after all."

"I don't just want to help people write grants. I come into my trust in a couple of months, and I wanted to—"

Logan strode into the living room. "Hey, you two! Dinner's ready."

"We'll be along in a minute," Lawrence said.

Laurel pushed to her feet. "Oh no. It's rude to keep the chef waiting. We'll finish talking about it after dinner, okay?"

Her brother glanced between them. "Everything okay?"

For the first time in a long time, she felt like it actually was.

She looped her arm through her brother's. "Everything's fine. Let's eat."

CHAPTER 15

*I*n the slightly less dark stretch before dawn, Sebastian watched Laurel sleep. No lines of strain marred that gorgeous face. Her chest rose and fell in a slow, easy rhythm. One of her legs threaded through his, and one hand pressed against his chest, as if she needed to know he was there, even in sleep. She always slept like this with him, and he loved it.

He wanted her. Again. That was pretty much a constant, and this was their last stretch of time this weekend. She had class at eight. He considered waking her, loving the body he'd come to know so well, but they'd already been up most of the night, wringing out as much pleasure as they could from their limited time together. She needed to be sharp for class and he needed to be sharp enough to drive back to Eden's Ridge. So he watched her instead, memorizing every millimeter of her face so he'd be able to call it up during the long-lonely nights ahead until the next weekend they managed to carve out.

Her eyes fluttered open, and her lips curved. That instant glow in her smile at the sight of him kicked Sebastian right in the chest. Christ, he was a lucky bastard.

He smoothed back her hair, still mussed from his hands. "Hi."

"Morning. What time is it?" That early morning voice rasped with sleep and sex and had his already hard cock making another bid for attention.

"About 6:30, I think."

She bolted up. "What? Shit. I should have been up half an hour ago. My alarm must not have gone off." Springing naked from the bed, she strode toward the bathroom. At the doorway, she glanced over her shoulder. "What are you waiting for?"

"Huh?" He was still distracted from the view.

"If you hurry, we can squeeze in one last quickie in the shower."

He beat her to the shower, wrenching on the water. As soon as it was warm, he dragged her beneath the spray, devouring her mouth and filling his hands with her body, still flushed from sleep. She rose to him, matching his hunger with her own as she wrapped her arms around his shoulders. His hand skated down the slope of her belly, between her thighs, to find her already wet and ready.

She tipped her hips into his hand. "Hurry."

He remembered their first night together, her fevered chant as he'd taken her apart. He didn't have time for that slow, methodical loving. *Next time*, he promised, as he lifted her up, pressing her against the shower wall and sliding into her, as the water beat down on them both. She cried out as he filled her, and Sebastian thought he'd never get tired of hearing her unabashed pleasure.

"Hurry," she gasped again.

He began to move, driving into her, drinking down every moan and cry as he lost himself in the heat they made together. She crested, coming so hard and fast, her orgasm yanked him over the edge, milking him until it was all he could do to keep them both upright.

Breathing hard, she pressed her brow to his. "Maybe that'll hold us until next time."

"I give it forty-eight hours. Maybe."

She laughed and reached for the shampoo.

By the time they were dressed, there was no time for breakfast. They each packed their respective bags, reaching out for more lingering touches.

"I'll be back on Thursday for delivery." Since she'd come back to school in January, he'd taken over the weekly Nashville delivery for Maxwell Organics, just for the chance to see her every week. Sometimes they managed a meal. Sometimes it was just fifteen minutes with her in his arms. Right now it was keeping them afloat.

Zipping her messenger bag, she wrapped her arms around him. "Just two more months until graduation. Then it'll be all me, all the time."

"Can't wait." He didn't know yet what their life together would look like.

They'd spent a lot of time since Christmas dreaming. Well, he thought of it as dreaming. Laurel considered it the first part of a multi-step action plan, with assorted variations, depending on which funding they ultimately got. She was a force to be reckoned with, and she'd made him not only see the possibilities but believe in them. With her help, they'd submitted three grant applications so far. They were still waiting to hear the results.

She reached for a sheaf of papers on her desk. "Before you go...I've got one more grant application."

"Another one?" When the hell had she found the time for more?

"I know, I know. But this one is for a new regional non-profit, so there won't be as much competition for funds. If you landed this one, it would be enough to buy Josiah Massey's place."

Sebastian went still. "By itself?"

"Yeah. With enough left over to at least get a solid start on repairs."

Massey's place was their white whale. Laurel's predictions on that front had been wholly accurate. The bank had it for sale, but so far there'd been no interest. They could only hope that continued to be the case until they could get all their ducks in a row. If this grant was really that big...

He sucked in a breath and let it out slow. "Okay. I'll take care of it." The grants, at least, gave him something to fill the empty evening hours with while he was missing her.

Handing over the application, she slid her arms around him. "Take care of you, too."

"I will. I promise." He shoved the paperwork in his bag and glanced at the clock. "You've got to go."

"I know. Walk me out to the car."

They loaded their respective bags and met in the middle.

He pulled her into his arms. "This never gets any easier."

"No. I gotta admit, though, I'm glad you're not in the Army anymore. I'm not sure I could hack it as a military girlfriend, with all those long deployments."

"I figure I'm right where I'm supposed to be. Finally."

She grinned. "Damn straight." Rising to her toes, she kissed him, drawing him in with her sweetness and still simmering heat.

Because he knew he had to, he pulled back. "You're gonna be late to class."

"Damn it. Okay." She let him go, stepping back and opening her car door. "See you soon. Talk tonight?"

"Absolutely. I love you."

"Love you, too."

She got into her Mini Cooper and blew him a kiss as she pulled out of the drive.

Sebastian watched until she was out of sight, feeling like the luckiest bastard on earth and wondering how a woman like her was truly into a guy like him. Then he smiled, knowing her response to that question would be some kind of fierce argument and probably taking him to bed to show him. Repeatedly.

Life was really fucking good.

Now he just had to be patient and get through the next eight weeks.

~

AT LONG LAST, it was over. Laurel was officially a graduate of Vanderbilt Law School. Number three in her class. She'd been hooded, congratulated by faculty and friends, and now she was wading through the chaos of the crowd on Curry Field, trying to find her family. It had rained last night, so she hadn't worn her heels on the sodden grass, and she cursed the fact that the DNA gods hadn't seen fit to pass on any of her father or brother's height. Maybe she should stand on one of the chairs set out under the big tent.

"Laurel!"

Turning, she spotted Sebastian, cutting through the crowd like a knife. Everything inside her lit up at the sight of him. So she was laughing as he scooped her up, spinning her in a circle.

"Hot damn, you did it!"

"Yes, I did! I missed you." She framed his face and kissed him hard and fast.

"There's our girl!" Beaming, her father broke through next, trailed by her mom, Logan, and Athena.

She got passed from one to the next. With every hug, every congratulations, it seemed another layer of the stress and anxiety that had lingered like a malaise finally began to lift. Joy and relief had her almost vibrating through all the requisite pictures. She was *finished*, and she could finally get started on the next phase of her life. But that necessitated a chance for some one-on-one conversation with Sebastian.

"Okay, I'm starting to bake in this cap and gown, and I'm absolutely starving. The graduate requests *food!*"

As the day belonged to her, she announced where she wanted to go, and everyone split up to take separate vehicles. Sebastian came with her. Laurel slipped her arm through his, happy for the chance to touch him.

"I'm proud of you, you know."

She tipped her head up to study his face. "Yeah?"

"Yeah. You figure out how to take your degree and make it work for you."

Her step hitched. Had someone told him and ruined the surprise? "Where there's a will, there's a way. And I've got a lot of will."

"It's one of the things I love about you."

They reached her car, and she stripped out of the cap, gown, and hood. Sebastian looked utterly ridiculous folded into the front passenger seat of her Mini.

"You'll be great at this grant-writing thing. I mean, how many did you help me submit this semester in the middle of everything else?"

"Six." Laurel swallowed, suddenly nervous as she backed out of the space. If she waited for him to bring it up, they'd lose this small window alone, and she couldn't trust someone not to spill the beans at lunch. "Shouldn't you have been hearing about the Calico Foundation grant this week?"

"Actually, I heard this morning. But today is for you. I didn't want to detract from that."

Exasperated, she shot him a look. "How would you getting the grant detract from that??? Today is for celebrating!"

His brows drew together. "How did you know I got the grant?"

"Of course you got it. It's my foundation." Her mouth snapped shut like a trap. That wasn't how she'd meant for that to come out.

"It's what now?"

Well, she was in it now. "Calico Foundation is the non-profit I set up with the money from my trust."

"What trust?" Was there suspicion in that neutral tone? She couldn't tell.

"My maternal grandparents left both Logan and me trusts that we gained access to when we turned twenty-five. It's how he could afford to buy the farm. This is what I decided to do with mine."

She chanced another glance in his direction and found him frowning.

"You set up a foundation just to fund my program?"

Disbelief was probably bad. She needed to salvage this situation. "Not just your program. I set up a foundation to provide grant funding for all sorts of regional projects. Things that will make life better for the people of Tennessee. Yours just happened to be the first one I chose to fund."

Sebastian sucked in a breath. "I—don't know what to say."

She couldn't read him, and it rattled her. Biting her lip, she tried to find a way to explain this that wasn't going to be a blow to his pride. "You were worried that you wouldn't be enough, that helping you with the therapy program wouldn't be enough for me. You were partly right. I want to make a difference, Sebastian. I *need* to make a difference. And this way I can, on a much broader scale, without ever having to leave Eden's Ridge or you."

She pulled into a parking space at the restaurant and turned to face him. His jaw was working and he wasn't looking at her. She laid a hand on his arm, needing to make him understand.

"Please don't be angry. I didn't decide to fund your program just because it was yours. I believe in what you can do with it. And I didn't tell you about it because I wasn't sure if you'd accept the money if you knew it was from me. I knew for sure you wouldn't if it came directly from me, so I got Dad to help me change the beneficiary of the trust to the Calico Foundation."

His gaze snapped back toward her. "Your dad knows about this?"

"Yeah. He specializes in estate planning, so he's the one who wrote the original trusts for my grandparents."

"And he didn't pitch a fit that you did this?"

"No." And hadn't that been a surprise? "He's pretty psyched

about my new direction and excited about the kinds of programs it could support. He was actually really impressed with your proposal."

Sebastian went quiet, his expression utterly blank.

Anxiety began to curl in her belly. She'd wanted to do a good thing for them both, but what if she'd overstepped? What if he couldn't accept what she brought to this? Had she ruined everything by setting this up behind his back?

"Please say something," she whispered.

Instead, he lunged across the seat, cupping her nape and dragging her mouth to his for a fierce kiss. "I love you. I love you so damned much. Thank you for doing this."

"You're...not mad?"

"I'm not mad. I'm in shock. You're the most generous, capable woman I've ever met. You could do literally anything with your life, and you're choosing me."

Relieved, she cupped his face, stroking a thumb across his cheek. "I know a good investment when I see it, and a life with you is at the top of my list."

"Thank God." He leaned in to kiss her again.

Somebody knocked on the window, and Laurel startled back in the seat.

From outside the car, Athena smirked. "Hey, if you two are done making out in the parking lot, we're all going inside to eat."

As her sister-in-law strolled on toward the restaurant, Laurel snickered. "For the record, I am never going to be done making out in the parking lot."

"Noted, counselor." Sebastian sobered. "I'm going to buy an entire farm."

"I'm going to run an entire charitable foundation."

"I need a burger."

"Dad's buying. Let's eat steak. And lobster."

"That's my girl."

EPILOGUE

1 YEAR LATER

"Careful." Sebastian and Ty eased up the front porch steps and set the whiskey barrel planter opposite its mate by the front door. The bright-faced impatiens nodded in the early May breeze, a nice contrast to the freshly-painted house.

Further down the porch, Harrison and Ivy hung the last of the massive Boston ferns from eye bolts in the eaves. In the yard, the last of Porter's crew packed up their trucks. It had been a whirl-wind week, taking advantage of the fact that Laurel was out of town, meeting with the board of the Calico Foundation to settle on this year's grant recipients. Sebastian had recruited all his friends to help him finally tackle the exterior of the old farmhouse.

After the funding came through, he and Laurel had moved in to Josiah Massey's place last summer. With the addition of the three smaller grants they'd received, there'd been enough to rehab the barn and get the therapy program solidly started. They'd managed all the basic repairs on the house, but the focus had necessarily been on the business. The business was thriving now. Felicity Harmon, their new therapist, had been a Godsend, allowing Sebastian to spend the majority of time on his rescues.

Now he was thinking toward the future. That meant taking the steps to give her the home she'd imagined all those months ago.

Looking at it now, he thought they'd pulled it off. The siding had been painted the blue-gray she'd described, with crisp white trim and new dark gray shutters. Window boxes he'd built with his own hands were mounted across the front of the house, multi-colored petunias spilling over the edges. At the far end, a big porch swing, with bright, overstuffed cushions—Ivy's contribution— hung looking out over the view of the barn and pastures beyond. Mr. Rochester had already taken ownership of that, curling up on one end and swishing his tail. They needed some kind of a table to put in front of it for that coffee and lemonade, but Laurel would probably want to pick that out herself.

As the last of Porter's crew pulled out of the drive, Sebastian cast a final look around. "That should do it. Thank y'all for all your help. I couldn't have pulled this off without you."

Harrison clapped him on the shoulder. "Happy you finally asked for help with something."

"See? And it didn't even kill you," Ty teased.

"I'm all about supporting love," Porter announced. "Congratulations, man."

"You can't congratulate me until she says yes."

"She's not gonna say no," Ivy insisted. "When is she supposed to be getting home?"

"Soon. Y'all need to vamoose." He tugged out his phone and pulled up her location. "She's—oh hell, she's a quarter mile away! They're early! There's no way you can get out of here without being seen. Scatter."

"Where?" Ty asked.

"I don't know! For fuck's sake go hide. Y'all weren't supposed to be here for this." Tunneling both hands through his hair, Sebastian reviewed the plan, wondering what needed to change.

His friends bolted for the barn. Maybe she wouldn't look down there. Maybe she'd just think it was the latest therapy clients. As long as Logan had the blindfold in place and Laurel was cooperating…

A truck turned in at the end of the drive. Logan's truck. Sebastian's palms went damp.

You got this.

They pulled up in front of the house. He checked to make sure the guys were hidden away, then circled around to open the passenger door.

"Why am I blindfolded?" Laurel demanded.

Lips quirking, he leaned in to brush a kiss to her cheek as he unbuckled her seatbelt. "Hello to you, too."

"Sebastian, what is going on?"

"A surprise."

"I'm not sure how I feel about surprises."

"You're going to like this one." God, he sure as hell hoped she did.

Taking her hands, he helped her out of the truck. Logan grabbed her suitcase from the back and deposited it by the steps.

"I'm gonna get on home to Athena. Welcome back, Pip." To Sebastian he mouthed, "Good luck," and climbed back in the truck.

As soon as he disappeared, Sebastian's tongue turned thick and clumsy. Feeling more than a little stupid, he blurted, "How was your trip?"

"Seriously? You've got me standing here blindfolded and you want to chat about my trip?"

"Okay, okay." It was time. He could do this.

Walking her out a little ways, he turned her to face the house, so she could get the full effect. "Welcome home, baby." With that, he slid off the blindfold.

Laurel gasped, bringing both hands to her mouth as her eyes went wide. "Sebastian!"

"I hope I got it right."

"It's perfect!"

He opened his mouth to speak, but she was already moving up the steps, running her hands over the freshly painted railing, the flowers in the barrels, the trailing ends of the ferns.

Christ this was happening so much faster than he'd planned. He hurried to catch up.

"And my swing!" As she rushed over to investigate it, he dropped down to one knee. "Sebastian, this is so—oh!"

Her legs seemed to go out from under her and she sat down hard on the swing, almost missing the seat entirely and narrowly avoiding the cat. Mr. Rochester yowled in protest and leapt down, disappearing around the edge of the house.

Swallowing hard, he tried to remember the speech he'd prepared. "Laurel, I think you know I love you."

Her lips quirked. "Yeah I've kinda had a suspicion."

Her tone of dry amusement eased some of the tension in his chest. "The first time we came here, you painted a picture of how you imagined the house, the grounds, the life that could be built here. Over the last year, we've come a long way toward bringing that picture to life, but there's still one piece missing. And it wasn't from what you described that day. It's from what I saw in my own head—getting to wake up every morning and come out here to have a cup of coffee with my wife before going to do the life's work she helped to make a reality."

He pulled the ring out of his pocket, grateful he'd taken to carrying it around for the last two weeks. "In all our time together, I've never asked you for anything. Asking has always been hard for me. But asking you this isn't hard, because I know, deep down, that it's exactly right. So what do you say to doing this last thing, making all this perfection official. Will you marry me?"

Her eyes shone and her smile was the brightest thing he'd ever seen. "There's nothing I want to do more."

Blowing out a breath, he rose and moved to slip the ring on her finger.

An explosion of cheers pulled their attention down to the barn, where the peanut gallery hadn't stayed in the barn.

"Sorry. They were supposed to be gone already. You got home early."

She looped her arms around his neck. "I couldn't wait to see you. And this is the best surprise ever. I love you."

"I love you, too." He kissed her, immediately sinking deeper and wishing he could cart her upstairs.

Easing back Laurel grinned up at him. "Let's go accept our congratulations and kick them out. We have some celebrating to do."

<hr />

Choose Your Next Romance

THE THIRD AND final installment of the Rescue My Heart trilogy will absolutely follow Ty finding his happily ever after. While you're waiting, have you checked out The Misfit Inn quartet? It begins with *When You Got A Good Thing*, Kennedy and Xander's story. This whole series is all about the family you make and the bonds between sisters, with plenty of Ari's matchmaking.

Can't decide? Keep turning the pages for a sneak peek!

WHEN YOU GOT A GOOD THING

THE MISFIT INN, BOOK #1

Charming, poignant, and sexy, *When You Got a Good Thing* **pulled me in with its sweet charm and deft storytelling, and didn't let go until the very last page. It has everything I love in a small-town romance!** ~USA **Today Best-Selling Author Tawna Fenske**

She thought she could never go home again. Kennedy Reynolds has spent the past decade traveling the world as a free spirit. She never looks back at the past, the place, or the love she left behind —until her adopted mother's unexpected death forces her home to Eden's Ridge, Tennessee.

Deputy Xander Kincaid has never forgotten his first love. He's spent ten long years waiting for the chance to make up for one bone-headed mistake that sent her running. Now that she's finally home, he wants to give her so much more than just an apology.

Kennedy finds an unexpected ally in Xander, as she struggles to mend fences with her sisters and to care for the foster child her mother left behind. Falling back into his arms is beyond tempting, but accepting his support is dangerous. He can never know the truth about why she really left. Will Kennedy be able to bury the past and carve out her place in the Ridge, or will her secret destroy her second chance?

 et your copy of *When You Got A Good Thing* today!

OTHER BOOKS BY KAIT NOLAN

A complete and up-to-date list of all my books can be found at https://kaitnolan.com.

~

THE MISFIT INN SERIES
SMALL TOWN FAMILY ROMANCE

- *When You Got A Good Thing* (Kennedy and Xander)
- *Til There Was You* (Misty and Denver)
- *Those Sweet Words* (Pru and Flynn)
- *Stay A Little Longer* (Athena and Logan)
- *Bring It On Home* (Maggie and Porter)

RESCUE MY HEART SERIES
SMALL TOWN MILITARY ROMANCE

- *Baby It's Cold Outside* (Ivy and Harrison)
- *What I Like About You* (Laurel and Sebastian)
- *Bad Case of Loving You* (Paisley and Ty prequel)

- *Made For Loving You* (Paisley and Ty)

MEN OF THE MISFIT INN
SMALL TOWN SOUTHERN ROMANCE

- *Let It Be Me* (Emerson and Caleb)
- *Our Kind of Love* (Abbey and Kyle)

WISHFUL SERIES
SMALL TOWN SOUTHERN ROMANCE

- *Once Upon A Coffee* (Avery and Dillon)
- *To Get Me To You* (Cam and Norah)
- *Know Me Well* (Liam and Riley)
- *Be Careful, It's My Heart* (Brody and Tyler)
- *Just For This Moment* (Myles and Piper)
- *Wish I Might* (Reed and Cecily)
- *Turn My World Around* (Tucker and Corinne)
- *Dance Me A Dream* (Jace and Tara)
- *See You Again* (Trey and Sandy)
- *The Christmas Fountain* (Chad and Mary Alice)
- *You Were Meant For Me* (Mitch and Tess)
- *A Lot Like Christmas* (Ryan and Hannah)
- *Dancing Away With My Heart* (Zach and Lexi)

WISHING FOR A HERO SERIES (A WISHFUL SPINOFF SERIES)
SMALL TOWN ROMANTIC SUSPENSE

- *Make You Feel My Love* (Judd and Autumn)
- *Watch Over Me* (Nash and Rowan)
- *Can't Take My Eyes Off You* (Ethan and Miranda)
- *Burn For You* (Sean and Delaney)

MEET CUTE ROMANCE

SMALL TOWN SHORT ROMANCE

- *Once Upon A Snow Day*
- *Once Upon A New Year's Eve*
- *Once Upon An Heirloom*
- *Once Upon A Coffee*
- *Once Upon A Campfire*
- *Once Upon A Rescue*

SUMMER CAMP
CONTEMPORARY ROMANCE

- *Once Upon A Campfire*
- *Second Chance Summer*

ABOUT KAIT

Kait is a Mississippi native, who often swears like a sailor, calls everyone sugar, honey, or darlin', and can wield a bless your heart like a saber or a Snuggie, depending on requirements.

You can find more information on this RITA ® Award-winning author and her books on her website http:// kaitnolan.com. While you're there, sign up for her newsletter so you don't miss out on news about new releases!

Lightning Source UK Ltd.
Milton Keynes UK
UKHW021555080621
385145UK00008B/1618

9 781648 350207